I0813934

GREAT DISCOVERIES IN SCIENCE

New Frontiers in Astronomy

by Elizabeth Schmermund

Cavendish Square
New York

Published in 2017 by Cavendish Square Publishing, LLC
243 5th Avenue, Suite 136, New York, NY 10016

First Edition

CPSIA Compliance Information: Batch #CS16CSQ

All websites were available and accurate when this book was sent to press.

Library of Congress Cataloging-in-Publication Data
Names: Schmermund, Elizabeth.
Title: New frontiers in astronomy / Elizabeth Schmermund.
Description: New York : Cavendish Square Publishing, [2017] | Series:
Great discoveries in science | Includes bibliographical references and index.
Identifiers: LCCN 2016009001 (print) | LCCN 2016016645 (ebook) |
ISBN 9781502619594 (library bound) | ISBN 9781502619600 (ebook)
Subjects: LCSH: Cosmology--Juvenile literature. | Astronomy--Juvenile
literature. | Dark matter (Astronomy)--Juvenile literature.
Classification: LCC QB983 .S36 2017 (print) | LCC QB983 (ebook) |
DDC 523.1--dc23
LC record available at https://lccn.loc.gov/2016009001

Editorial Director: David McNamara
Editor: Caitlyn Paley
Copy Editor: Michele Suchomel-Casey
Art Director: Jeffrey Talbot
Designer: Joseph Macri
Production Assistant: Karol Szymczuk
Photo Research: J8 Media

The photographs in this book are used by permission and through the courtesy of: NASA/SDO and the AIA, EVE, and HMI science teams, cover; NASA/JPL-Caltech, 4; NASA, ESA, and D. Coe, 8; New York Public Library/Science Source/Getty Images, 10; Science Source, 14; David McNew/Getty Images, 17; AP Images, 22; NASA/WMAP Science Team, 26, 77; Fred Stein Archive/Archive Photos/Getty Images, 28; posteriori/Shutterstock.com, 31; Science & Society Picture Library/Getty Images, 35; ESO/WFI (Optical)/MPIfR/ESO/APEX/A.Weiss et al. (Submillimetre)/NASA/CXC/CfA/R.Kraft et al. (X-ray), 36; GIPhotoStock/Science Source/Getty Images, 42; Huntington Library/Superstock, 46; John Irwin Collection/AIP/Science Source, 53; chrisjo/iStock, 55; Holger Motzkau/Wikimedia Commons, 58, 61; John D. and Catherine T. MacArthur Foundation/Wikimedia Commons, 59; Stocktrek Images/Thinkstock, 62; Fineart1/Shutterstock.com, 68; European Space Agency/Wikimedia Commons, 73; shooarts/Shutterstock.com, 75; Mehau Kulyk/Science Source, 79; Maximilien Brice/CERN, 83; ESA/C. Carreau, 84; Kimberly White/Breakthrough Prize/Getty Images, 86; ESA/Hubble & NASA, 93; Sloan Digital Sky Survey Team/NASA/NSF/DOE, 97.

Printed in the United States of America

Contents

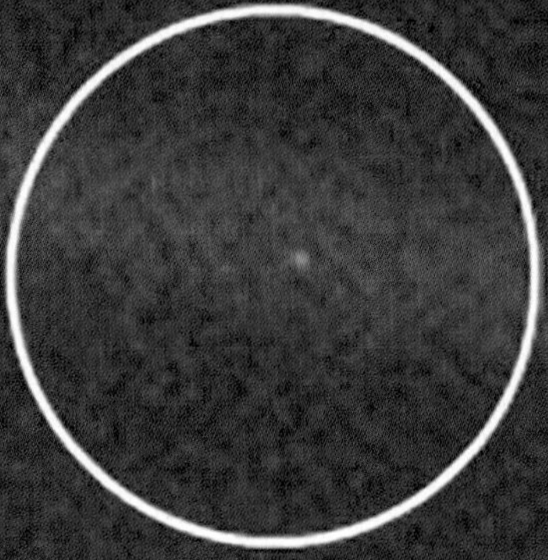

This blown-up image shows Earth (*circled*) as a "pale blue dot" in the enormity of space and was taken by the Voyager 1 space probe before it forever exited our solar system.

Introduction: Our Evolving Understanding of the Universe

For many thousands of years, humans have turned their eyes to the sky and asked questions that get to the root of who we are and where we come from. No other scientific exploration has captured our imaginations as the quest to understand our universe has. Although the visible features of the universe are farther than the human mind can imagine, we feel uniquely and inextricably connected with the cosmic. Scientists and artists together have tried to understand the universe in order to better comprehend themselves. As Joni Mitchell famously sings, "we are stardust, we are golden, we are billion-year-old carbon." The universe, in a very real way, is the source of every atom in our bodies.

Since the dawn of time, humans have been guided by the stars. In fact, astronomy is the oldest natural science, and its history is inextricable from the history of humankind. In prehistory, when humans were entirely dependent on the course of the seasons, celebrations were almost certainly held on solstices, when the days are the longest or shortest of the year. Many archaeologists and historians believe that monuments and henges—the most famous, of course, being Stonehenge in Wiltshire, England—were built as tribute to the movement of visible celestial bodies. In ancient Mesopotamia, religion was linked with the study of astronomy. This is where the foundation of our modern study of astronomy was developed. There, priest-astronomers observed the night sky in order to prophesy or divine, and the stars held answers to their most perplexing questions. Stars and constellations were catalogued as early as 1200 BCE—approximately two thousand years after linguists believe language developed. These early astronomers could identify some stars and planets, charted the movements of Venus among other planets, and observed and studied lunar and solar eclipses. Many years later, the Greeks would borrow from this ancient culture as they continued to study the stars.

One of the most important inventions in the history of the world is the **astrolabe**, an astronomical device invented in ancient Greece that many claim was the world's first computer. This intricate invention enabled astronomers and navigators to locate the positions of the sun, moon, planets, and stars, thus allowing for accurate predictions about sunrise and sunset as well as simply telling time. The astrolabe allowed explorers to travel to far-flung regions of the earth as it could determine longitude and latitude, and it was in use until the seventeenth century, when more advanced technology won out.

Then, in the fifteenth and sixteenth centuries, a new astronomical revolution swept across the world. Nicolaus Copernicus postulated a new model of the universe that, unlike the Greeks, placed the sun at the center of the universe, instead of Earth. This was a watershed moment in astronomy, although knowledge of the greater universe was still limited. Johannes Kepler and Galileo Galilei expanded on Copernicus's theories, revolutionizing the science of astronomy. Galileo, in particular, is known as the father of modern observational astronomy. He was one of the first scientists to peer at celestial bodies through a telescope, including the planet Neptune, which was only officially discovered some two hundred years later. Another, larger scientific revolution began in 1687 with the publication of Isaac Newton's *Naturalis Principia Mathematica*, which provided a mathematical basis for astronomical phenomena and would lay the groundwork for the combination of physics and astronomy, which we today call astrophysics.

But some of the most exciting astronomical discoveries to occur in several hundred years have occurred relatively recently. In 1915, a man named Albert Einstein developed the general theory of relativity, which drew upon Newton's insights to produce a theory of gravity as a property of space and time. This was one of the most significant scientific breakthroughs in the modern era and ushered in a new age of scientific observation, discovery, and understanding. But there were lots of exciting discoveries being made in the field of astronomy during this time. Edwin Hubble's observations in the Mount Wilson Observatory in California—aided by new advancements in photography—proved that our Milky Way galaxy was one of countless other galaxies in a seemingly chaotic universe. Soon after, astronomers such as Vesto Slipher provided calculations that proved that the universe was expanding rapidly. This laid the groundwork for George Lemaître's big bang theory, which has proved to be another watershed moment in our understanding of our universe and its origins.

Today, astronomers are still working hard to better understand our universe. We now know that our universe is not only expanding millions of years following its original propulsion during the big bang—it is accelerating. Astronomers and physicists have discovered that our accelerating universe is filled with a strange and invisible substance called dark matter and that its propulsion is directed by dark energy. Dark matter and dark energy together make up 95 percent of all the matter in our universe. This means

Today's physicists and astronomers investigate mysteries of the universe like dark matter.

that astronomers today still have a lot of work to do to better understand our universe—and, more importantly, that we stand at the threshold of another important moment in history where scientific discovery can completely change how we view ourselves and our surroundings.

In 1990, after the Voyager 1 space probe turned around to take one last photo of our planet before leaving our solar system forever, astronomer Carl Sagan reflected on the well-known image of our Earth as a tiny "pale blue dot" in an expanse of darkness. Sagan wrote:

> Look again at that dot. That's here. That's home. That's us. On it everyone you love, everyone you know, everything you ever heard of, every human being who ever was, lived out their lives. The aggregate of our joy and suffering, thousands of confident religions, ideologies, and economic doctrines, every hunter and forager, every hero and coward, every creator and destroyer civilization, every king and peasant, every young couple in love, every mother and father, hopeful child, inventor and explorer, every teacher of morals, every corrupt politician, every "superstar," every "supreme leader," every saint and sinner in the history of our species lived there—on a mote of dust suspended in a sunbeam.

This is where the continued quest for knowledge about the universe takes us.

The astronomer Edwin Hubble looks through a telescope at Palomar Observatory near San Diego, California.

CHAPTER 1

The Problem of a Changing Universe

Edwin Hubble was a precocious child who, nonetheless, exceled more at sports than academics. Born in 1889 in Marshfield, Missouri, Hubble initially planned to study law to please his father. Luckily, while teaching high school in Indiana in his mid-twenties, Hubble resolved to follow his lifelong dream of becoming a professional astronomer. The field of astronomy would never be the same.

After achieving his doctorate at the University of Chicago—and then joining the war effort against Germany until 1919—Hubble began observations at the largest telescope in the world: the 100-inch (254-centimeter) Hooker telescope at Mount Wilson Observatory in Los Angeles, California. Over two clear nights in October 1923, Hubble took forty-minute exposures of the Andromeda **galaxy**. The Andromeda galaxy, we now know, is the closest major grouping of stars, gas, and dust to our Milky Way galaxy. However, during this time, astronomers did not know what a galaxy was—or if there were any groupings of stars outside of our own area in space.

After observing the plates, Hubble made an important discovery: there was a **Cepheid variable star** visible on one of the arms of the Andromeda spiral. Hubble wrote "VAR!"

across the plate. Cepheid variables are large stars that change brightness at predictable rates. Due in part to this **pulsation pattern**, Cepheid variables are very useful for astronomers to calculate distances. (This was a discovery originally made by the important, but often overlooked, female astronomer Henrietta Swan Leavitt in 1908.) This means that the light emitted from these stars pulses at a predictable rate; using a Cepheid variable's **luminosity** and the time in between pulses, astronomers can accurately calculate how far the star is from Earth.

That night in 1923, Edwin Hubble used his observations of the Cepheid variable to calculate its distance from Earth. What he found would revolutionize our understanding of astronomy forever. The star was way too far away to be part of our own galaxy, the Milky Way. That meant that it was in another galaxy, thousands of light-years away. Hubble understood the significance of his discovery right away: our galaxy was not the only galaxy in the universe. With the discovery of this one Cepheid variable, our universe grew to an almost unimaginable size.

OUR GROWING UNIVERSE

Before Edwin Hubble's exciting discovery, astronomers had limited knowledge of anything outside of our solar system. In 1785, the astronomer William Herschel attempted to map the Milky Way as an elliptical shape with our own solar system at the center. In fact, before this, many astronomers believed that **nebulae**, as these celestial objects that Hubble observed were called, lay within our own Milky Way galaxy.

In the early twentieth century, there was much disagreement over whether the Milky Way was the only galaxy in the universe. This disagreement was epitomized by a publically held debate between the famous astronomers Harlow Shapley and Heber Curtis in 1920, called "**the Great**

Debate." The reason for this division within the astronomical community was due to recent developments in technology that allowed telescopes to see objects at greater distances—leading astronomers to begin to ask new questions about the size and structure of our universe.

The Great Debate

As more technologically advanced telescopes were built and these nebulae became visible, some scientists, such as Shapley, argued that the universe consisted entirely of the Milky Way galaxy. He, and many others, believed that it was a matter of common sense. If these celestial objects were not part of our galaxy, then they would have to be extremely far away—on the order of 10^8 light-years. This means that it would take one hundred million years for something traveling at the **speed of light** to reach these objects. For many scientists, including Shapley, this was impossible—and laughable. The universe simply could not be that big.

Curtis, however, believed that these nebulae were, in fact, distant galaxies. Curtis and others pointed to the fact that it seemed like there were more novae, or exploding **white dwarf stars**, in Andromeda than in the Milky Way. If these nebulae were part of our galaxy, then why would so many novae occur in such a small section and not across the wider Milky Way?

Curtis also pointed to the significant **Doppler shift** of the nebulae. The nebulae showed redshift, which signified that they were moving away from Earth at higher speeds than the stars around them. Why would the nebulae, if they were part of our galaxy, be moving faster than both us and the stars around them?

The debate, which previously had taken place largely in scientific publications, finally occurred on April 26, 1920, at the Smithsonian Museum of Natural History. Curtis and

Harlow Shapley, an American astronomer who argued against Heber Curtis during the Great Debate in 1920 that the universe consisted entirely of the Milky Way galaxy

The Doppler Effect

The Doppler effect, as applied to astronomy, was discovered in 1912 by Vesto Slipher, who used a **spectrograph**, or an instrument used to measure the wavelengths in electromagnetic radiation, to determine that the nebulae were moving away from Earth at incredible speeds. The Doppler effect is the name for the phenomenon in which the frequency of a wave, such as light, changes as it moves toward or away from a point in space. The visible light of one of these celestial objects can shift either toward the red end of the spectrum or the blue end of the spectrum, depending on if it is moving closer or farther away from us. If it shifts toward the red, this is called redshift and signifies that the object is increasing in wavelength and moving away from us. As an object moves closer to us, its wavelengths get shorter and the light moves closer to the blue end of the spectrum, which is called blueshift.

Shapley argued their positions in front of a large audience. But the questions raised by both sides would not be fully answered until Edwin Hubble's important discovery three years later.

Hubble's Galaxies

Soon after Hubble's discovery, he contacted Shapley and told him that, following his measurements, the Cepheid in what we know today as the Andromeda galaxy must be around a million light-years from Earth. Shapley was surprised but conceded that he had lost the Great Debate. In fact, Shapley had rightly estimated the size of the Milky Way galaxy but had been wrong about the size of the universe—which was immeasurably large. Even Hubble would end up underestimating the distance between Andromeda and Earth. More than twenty years later, the German astronomer Walter Baade would show, using a recalculation using the periods of the Cepheid in Andromeda, that the galaxy is closer to two million light-years away from us.

Just five years later, Hubble had photographed and documented many galaxies. In fact, he observed so many galaxies that he had to begin a classification system to organize them. Hubble created this system based on the shape of galaxies in which every observable galaxy would fit. Spiral galaxies have a bulge in the center from which spiral arms spread out. Barred spiral galaxies have stars arranged in a bar shape that cut across the center of the spiral-shaped galaxy. Elliptical galaxies are shaped like a smooth ellipse without arms. Any galaxy that does not fall into one of the previous categories is called, according to Hubble's system, an **irregular galaxy**.

But Hubble's work was not yet done. In 1926, Hubble decided that he wanted to calculate the size of the universe—so much larger, it seemed, than astronomers had thought previous to Hubble's work with galaxies. Hubble thought that observing redshifts would allow him to do this work. He decided to find

The moon rises over Mount Wilson Observatory in Los Angeles, California.

Cepheids—the periodically pulsating stars so important in his previous work—in the farthest galaxies that he could find. With his colleague Milton Humason, he took a photograph over two nights at the Mount Wilson Observatory. Then, he studied this photo to determine the amount of redshift. Hubble then took photos of other galaxies and noted their redshifts. Because of his work with Cepheids, he knew which galaxies were closer to Earth and which were farther away. He would use this information to calibrate the redshift of galaxies.

What Hubble discovered from this experiment would soon be called **Hubble's law**. Hubble's law states that objects in deep space show redshifts, which are interpreted as rapid movement away from Earth. It also states that the celestial objects' velocity calculated from this redshift is directly proportional to their velocity. What this means is that Hubble's observation proved that everything in the universe is moving rapidly away from Earth.

This was another major discovery. It was the first evidence that the universe, which was recently thought to contain only our galaxy, was expanding. Hubble published a paper making this claim in 1929. Soon after, Albert Einstein, who had been working on the assumption that the universe was static and therefore not expanding or contracting as was the accepted belief at the time, abandoned his mathematical work in response to Hubble's discovery. He spent years reworking his general theory of relativity to allow for an expanding universe. Later, Einstein called his belief in a constant universe his biggest mistake and personally visited Hubble to thank him for his contribution to observational astronomy.

The AGE of the UNIVERSE

Over the next several years, Hubble's discovery was tested by other astronomers and shown to be correct. The idea that our universe is expanding became accepted fact. But this was only the beginning in a chain of exciting breakthroughs. Due to Hubble's work, astronomers soon realized they would be able to calculate the age of the universe by reversing the velocity of these galaxies and calculating backward to find out when they were all in the same place.

Calculating the age of the universe—as well as learning that our enormous universe was accelerating at a rapid pace—would have been unthinkable merely decades earlier. Hubble's discoveries had overturned the scientific community's understanding of our universe—and even provoked Einstein to tweak his general theory of relativity. According to Lawrence M. Krauss: "As far as the scientific community in 1917 was concerned, the universe was static and eternal, and consisted of a one single galaxy, our Milky Way, surrounded by vast, infinite dark, and empty space." By 1929, our knowledge of the universe and everything in it would be turned upside down.

But this doesn't mean that Hubble's work was extraordinarily hard or mathematically complicated. In fact, the beauty of his discovery was that, once he photographed these distant Cepheid variables, it was relatively easy to calculate their distance from Earth and, then, using multiple distances, calculate the age of the entire universe.

The Carnegie Institute for Science illustrates how "straightforward" these calculations are with the following example: "[I]magine that people are traveling home from a party. Consider two of the party guests traveling at 50 miles per hour [80 kilometers per hour] in opposite directions. If they are currently 100 miles [161 km] apart, how long ago did the party occur?"

The answer is that both guests left the party only one hour previous. While this example is extremely simplified, scientists used the same basic principle to calculate when all of the galaxies in the universe were clumped together at the party, so to speak.

Hubble calculated the age of the universe based on his measurements, but his number was low and not accurate. This was because his distance measurements had been off—the galaxies he had observed and calculated their distance from Earth based on redshift were much farther away than he believed them to be. Hubble passed away in 1953, without ever accurately calculating the age of the universe. However, one of his graduate students, Allan Sandage would continue his work.

In 1958, Sandage calculated the rate of expansion of the universe, called the **Hubble constant**. He noted that the reason why Hubble had not been able to come to this number was due to miscalculations, not due to Hubble's own mistakes, but rather due to the limited technology to which he had access at the time. This rate of expansion was a necessary step to calculate the age of the universe, similar to stating, in the example above, that the partygoers were traveling at a constant speed of 50 miles per hour (80 kmh).

Sandage also proved that the universe was much larger than even Hubble thought. His new calculations showed that the Andromeda galaxy was actually two million light-years away from Earth. Sandage's discovery was also revelatory. If Hubble had quite literally expanded scientists' understanding of the size and scope of our universe, Sandage doubled Hubble's calculations. He showed that Hubble's calculations were too low and the large universe he postulated was even larger in real life.

At that time, Sandage calculated that the age of the universe was fifteen billion years. He spent much of his life readjusting this number and claiming that the age of the universe must be older than he had originally calculated. This was because astronomers had miscalculated the age of certain stars during Sandage's lifetime, stating that these stars were older than the age of the universe! This, obviously, could not be true and led Sandage to doubt his own results. However, eventually, these stars were determined to be much younger than originally thought and Sandage's calculations were determined to be incredibly accurate. Today, scientists place the age of the universe at around 13.7 billion years.

The BIRTH of the BIG BANG

In 1927, a young Belgian astronomer and Catholic priest named Georges Lemaître published a paper in a little-known scientific journal that provided mathematical equations showing how Einstein's theory of general relativity could allow for an expanding universe. This had previously been accomplished in 1922 by a Russian mathematician named Alexander Friedmann, but Lemaître was able to see the connection between Hubble's recent work proving that the Milky Way was but one galaxy in our vast universe. Using Hubble's discovery, Lemaître realized that he could create a model of the universe according to general relativity. The problem that Lemaître saw was that Einstein's universe was static, although filled with matter, and another model of the universe (theorized by an astronomer and mathematician named Willem de Sitter) could allow for expansion but was completely empty. Lemaître imagined that he could create an accurate model of the universe as one that was both expanding and filled with matter; he said that this would "combine the advantages" of both Einstein's and de Sitter's models. His 1927 paper, which appeared before Hubble's observations, showed a cosmological model in which the universe is expanding and galaxies drift from the center. It received almost no attention at the time of its publication. In 1930, with Hubble's discovery, Lemaître drew attention to his paper and pointed out that it provided a model that backed up Hubble's observations. According to some scholars, the enormity of Hubble's discovery was not even understood until Lemaître's cosmological model was found and applied to it.

It would be Lemaître who would later declare, in 1931, that there must have been a moment when all of the galaxies in the universe had occupied the same space before being thrust outward. He theorized that the galaxies must have been densely packed together at this point in time. He described a "primeval atom" or a "cosmic egg, exploding at the moment of creation," and theorized that the instability of this atom must have provoked a great explosion that caused the matter to be thrust outward, causing our universe to continue expanding today. This, of course, would be the first scientific inquiry into the beginning of our universe and the theory of the big bang. But, when Lemaître first postulated this great explosion at the birth of our universe, he was not taken seriously. Even Einstein spoke out against this theory. He told Lemaître, "Your calculations are correct, but your physical insight is abominable." Lemaître, as a newcomer to astronomy who was often criticized for not having the correct credentials, grew frustrated at what he saw as experienced astronomers who refused to open up their minds to new theories. He retorted that Einstein was "not current with the astronomical facts."

Albert Einstein (*left*) and Georges Lemaître (*right*) had some disagreements over the moment of the creation of our universe, but eventually Einstein realized the importance of Lemaître's work.

In a short article entitled "The Beginning of the World from the Point of View of Quantum Theory," which appeared in the journal *Nature* following criticisms from fellow astronomers, Lemaître wrote:

> If we go back in the course of time … we find all the energy of the universe packed in a few or even in a unique quantum [the smallest amount of energy] … If this suggestion is correct, the beginning of the world happened a little before the beginning of space and time. I think that such a beginning of the world is far enough from the present order of Nature to be not at all repugnant … We could conceive the beginning of the universe in the form of a unique atom, the atomic weight of which is the total mass of the universe. This highly unstable atom would divide in smaller and smaller atoms by a kind of super-radioactive process.

It took not only Lemaître's genius, but also his creativity, to come up with such an incredible birth story for our universe. And, even more incredible, he was right.

The Big Bang's Detractors

Like many other astronomical theories, the big bang (coined only in 1949 by astronomer Fred Hoyle who used it to describe a theory he strongly disagreed with at the time) would be argued against and then forgotten before being revised and reanimated by other, later, scientists.

One of the reasons why many astronomers disagreed with Lemaître's theory for so long was because some people viewed an initial explosion as having religious undertones. These astronomers were fearful that pointing to a specific origin of the universe would import religious beliefs onto the science of astronomy by suggesting that there may be a "creator" of the universe as well as a moment of creation. These fears were compounded by the fact that Georges Lemaître was a Catholic priest. However, Lemaître himself stated that he would not, and could not, mix up scientific and religious belief. He stated:

> As far as I can see, such a theory remains entirely outside any metaphysical or religious question. It leaves the materialist free to deny any transcendental Being … For the believer, it removes any attempt at familiarity with God … It is consonant with Isaiah speaking of the hidden God, hidden even in the beginning of the universe.

Another reason was due to Hubble's miscalculations based on earlier, and less accurate, technology. Hubble's estimation that the universe was merely two billion years old did not make sense if the age of some stars was closer to ten billion years old and Earth's crust, according to geologic evidence, was three billion years old.

This would not be settled until Walter Baade recalculated Hubble's distances based on his observations of two different kinds of Cepheid stars, which had different levels of luminosity, or brightness. Hubble had only based his calculations on one type of Cepheid variable star.

According to a speech given by the astronomer Willem de Sitter in 1931, "Never in all the history of science…has there been a period when new theories and hypotheses arose, flourished, and were abandoned in so quick succession as in the last fifteen or twenty years." Author Marcia Bartusiak explains it in a different way:

> It took only three short decades—from 1900 to 1930, virtual seconds into our past when weighed against

humanity's life span—to make this mind-altering transition. The Milky Way, once the universe's lone inhabitant floating in an ocean of darkness, was suddenly joined by billions of other star-filled islands, arranged outward as far as telescopes could peer. Earth turned out to be less than a speech, the cosmic equivalent of a subatomic particle hovering within an immensity still difficult to grasp. It didn't stop there. Astronomers barely had time to adjust to this astounding celestial vastness when they were faced with the knowledge that space-time, the universe's very fabric, was expanding in all directions, carrying the galaxies with it. It was a rapid one-two punch from which astronomy is still reeling, as observers and theorists alike try to make sense of all its details: how the Big Bang was ignited, how the myriad galaxies were born and evolve, how (and if) the expansion will end.

Proof of the Big Bang

While many astronomers continued to prefer the model of the steady universe throughout the 1930s and 1940s, a Ukrainian-American physicist and cosmologist named George Gamow advocated the expanding universe model following Lemaître. As a physicist, he wanted to understand the conditions of the big bang. He imagined that due to the density of the big bang it had to be incredibly hot. Thus, he theorized that it was filled with radiation instead of matter. In 1948, Gamow published a paper, entitled "The Origin of Chemical Elements," with his student Ralph Adler. In this paper, he explained how the conditions of the big bang could account for the amount of hydrogen and helium in our universe, which account together for more than 99 percent of all matter. In this paper, Gamow

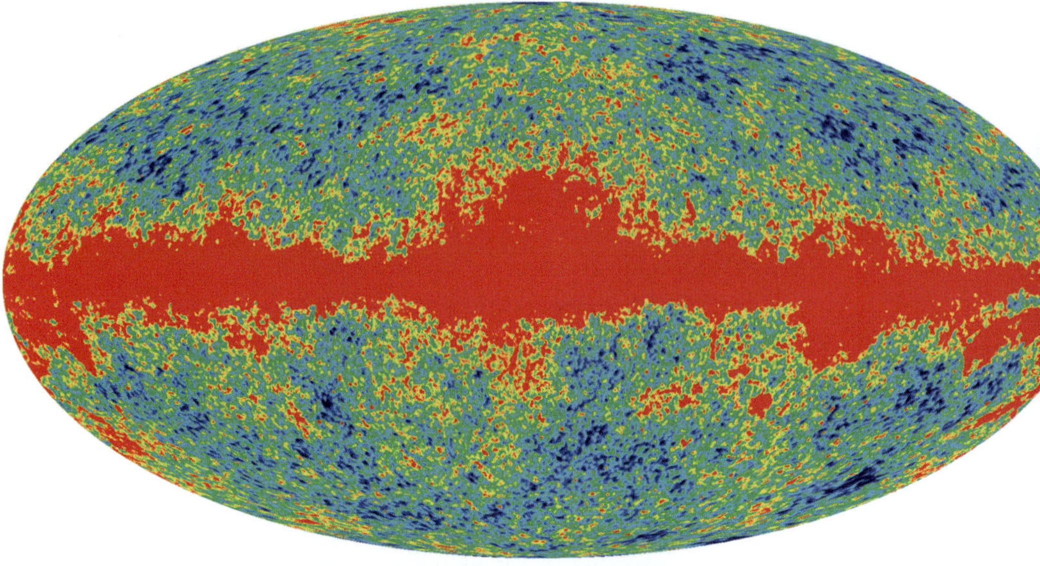

Created with data collected by the Wilkinson Microwave Anisotropy Probe (WMAP), this map shows fluctuations in cosmic microwave temperatures, remnants of the big bang.

and Adler also predicted the existence of **cosmic microwave background radiation (CMB)**. This is radiation left over from the Big Bang that radiated out and cooled, leaving the temperature of the universe at about five degrees above absolute zero.

In 1964, two radio astronomers, Arno Penzias and Robert Woodrow Wilson, accidentally discovered a strange background radiation, which appeared as a low and steady noise over their radio receiver. It wouldn't go away and continued day and night. The astronomers knew that the source of this noise was coming from outside of our own galaxy. This was the cosmic microwave background radiation that Gamow had predicted and became the first definitive proof of the existence of the big bang. Penzias and Wilson's observations had backed up the theoretical work done by Gamow, Lemaître, and Hubble.

In 1966, Lemaître was near death when he was handed the journal in which Penzias and Wilson's discovery of CMB was published. He died shortly after reading that the radiation he had theorized many years ago had been discovered—thus proving the big bang. In 1978, Penzias and Wilson won the Nobel Prize for Physics for their discovery.

Even Einstein would come around in regard to the importance of Lemaître's theoretical work. According to some sources, years after originally criticizing Lemaître's ideas, he would state, "This is the most beautiful and satisfactory explanation of creation to which I have ever listened."

But despite the discoveries that would signal the beginning of **cosmology**, the branch of astronomy that focuses on the beginning and evolution of the universe, astronomers still knew relatively little about the structure of the universe. A deeper understanding of space and the celestial objects it contains would continue to develop—but none of this would be possible without the calculations of the most brilliant man of his time, a theoretical physicist named Albert Einstein.

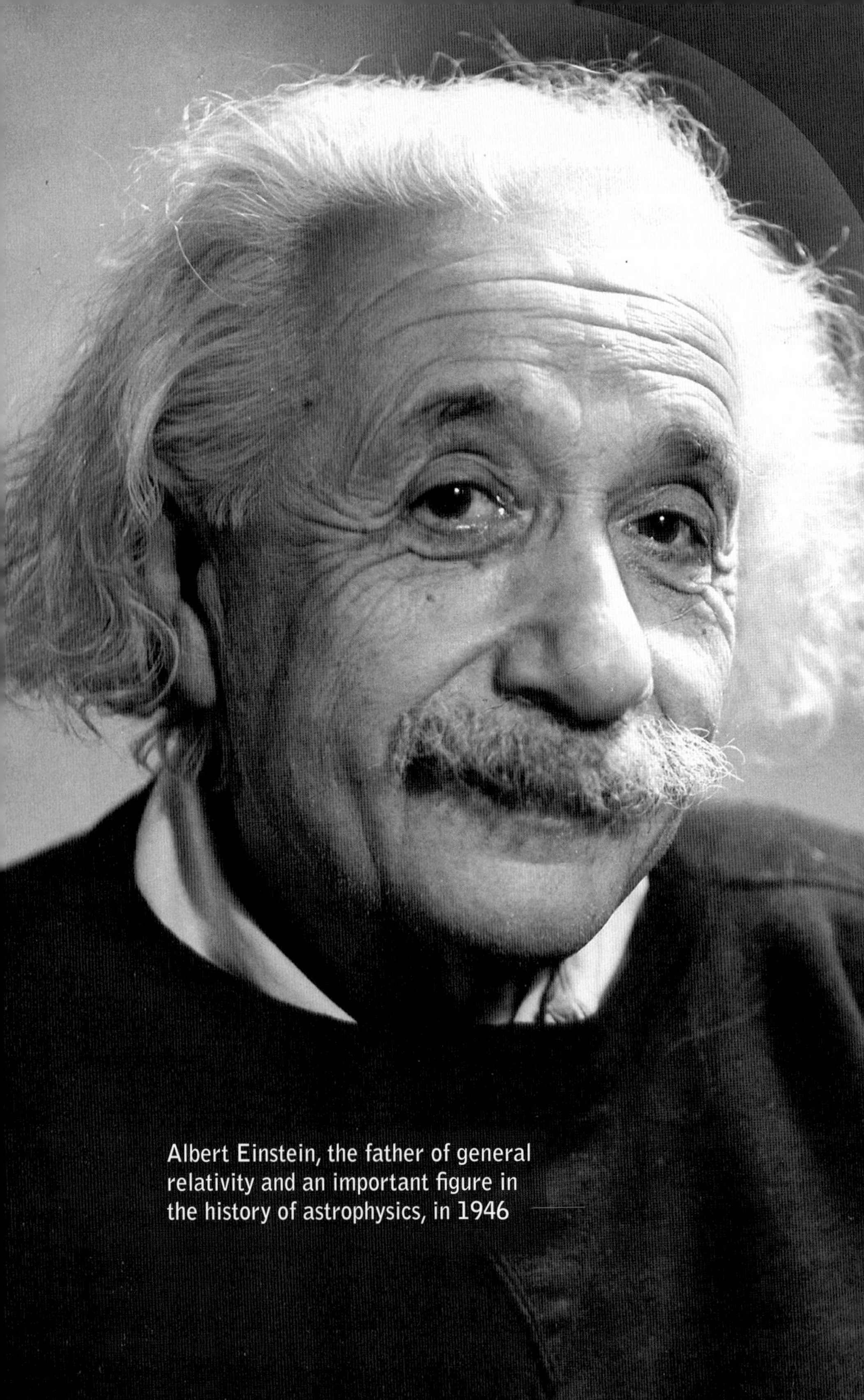

Albert Einstein, the father of general relativity and an important figure in the history of astrophysics, in 1946

CHAPTER 2

The Science of Cosmology

We would still be in the dark about our universe, so to speak, if not for Albert Einstein. Albert Einstein needs little introduction, but his theory of general relativity is less well known.

Albert Einstein was born in 1879 in the Kingdom of Württemberg in Germany. There are many rumors about Einstein's youth and academic aptitude. What we do know is that he criticized the lack of creativity and focus on memorization in his early studies and failed to gain entrance into the Swiss Federal Institute of Technology in Zurich, Switzerland, at the age of sixteen. However, he was a very good student, especially in math and physics, and passed the test the following year.

Albert Einstein, of course, would earn the reputation of being one of the smartest figures in history. As Isaac Newton had revolutionized science in the seventeenth century, so, too, would Einstein revolutionize physics with his general theory of relativity and quantum mechanics.

EINSTEIN'S GENERAL THEORY of RELATIVITY

Einstein devised his theory of relativity as a response to what he viewed as the limitations of Isaac Newton's system of gravity. In Newton's system, space was a blank field upon which forces, such as gravity, played. However, there were problems with Newtonian gravity, especially in regard to the forces between celestial objects. Newton's calculations did not correctly predict certain planets' orbits, such as Mercury. Another, bigger problem was that, according to Newton, a change in distance would immediately affect gravitational force. For example, with Newton's famous apple that falls from the tree, as the apple gets closer to the earth, it accelerates due to the increasing gravitational force acting upon the apple. But Einstein knew that this wouldn't be true with very large objects, such as planets or stars, which were millions of light-years apart. The change of the force of gravity between these two distant objects couldn't occur immediately because it would have to occur faster than the speed of light, which Einstein believed was impossible!

In order to solve these problems, Einstein had to rework Newtonian gravitation and rethink his understanding of space and time—using mathematical equations, of course. In order to make Newtonian gravity plausible, space could not just be the backdrop for the forces that play upon it. Rather, space had to become dynamic, changing according to any matter and energy that it contained. Quite simply: Einstein theorized that mass and energy can bend space. But Einstein also theorized that space is intimately related with time because of the way it is dynamically altered by the matter it contains. He theorized "**space-time**" as the interaction between space and time, and another dimension.

Scholars compare the way mass bends space to a heavy ball laying on a mattress or a rubber sheet. In this thought experiment, "[c]onsider the Sun sitting in space-time, imagined as a ball sitting on a rubber sheet. It curves the spacetime around it into a bowl shape. The planets orbit around the Sun because they are rolling across through this distorted space-time, which curves their motions like those of a ball rolling around inside a shallow bowl."

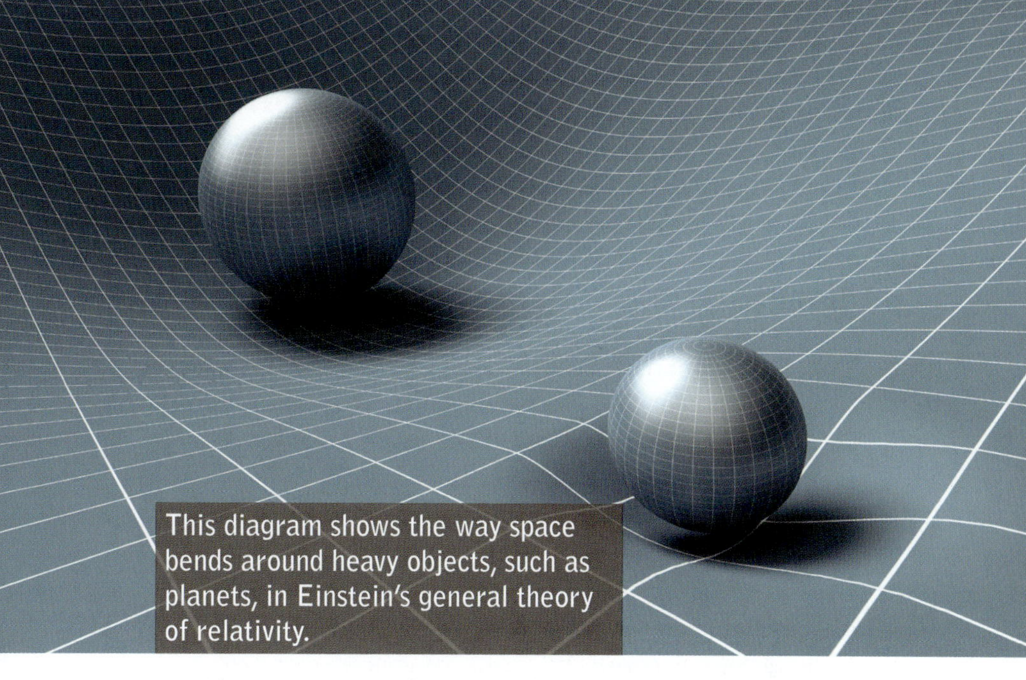

This diagram shows the way space bends around heavy objects, such as planets, in Einstein's general theory of relativity.

Thus, space is not flat and unchanging as Newton imagined, but a responsive dimension that both responds to matter within it and exerts force on that matter. Or, as the physicist John Wheeler wrote, "Matter tells space how to curve. Space[time] tells matter how to move."

Special Relativity

Einstein first published his theory of general relativity in 1915. But he had been working on it for many, many years. Ten years earlier, he had published on something he called "special relativity," which was a less generalized theory as to the way energy and space interact. According to special relativity, observers from any point in space who experience the same law of physics, as long as they aren't accelerating, will still measure the speed (the time it takes for an object to travel a certain distance) and mass of the object they are observing differently.

This is where Einstein's famous equation $E=mc^2$ comes from. In this equation, E stands for energy, m stands for mass, and c is the speed of light in a **vacuum**, which is a constant at 3.00 x 10^8 m/s, or 300,000,000 meters per second. Thus, the energy in a given system is equal to the mass it contains multiplied by the speed of light multiplied by itself (which is a very large number!). Before Einstein's theory of relativity, energy and mass were not seen as relative to one another and it was not known that mass could be converted to energy and vice versa. Although they seem different to us, mass and energy are treated by the laws of physics as the same thing—and Einstein was the first to show this. This equation shows also that, very simply, if mass decreases, energy will decrease as well. If energy decreases, mass will have to decrease as well.

The reason why the speed of light is included in this equation is because energy must travel at the speed of light. Light is a form of energy. When mass is converted to energy, then that energy will always travel at 300,000,000 meters per second in a vacuum (an accelerating or decelerating object, which is affected by other forces, is not treated by this simplified equation here). The reason why this number is multiplied by itself in Einstein's equation is because when something moves twice as fast as itself, it actually creates four times the energy. This means that even very small objects contain massive amounts of energy—the key is converting this mass into energy.

EINSTEIN'S THEORIES APPLIED

The understanding that an incredible amount of energy can be released by objects with relatively little mass is one of the most powerful consequences of Einstein's theory of special relativity. But there were many more tangible consequences to Einstein's work. Predictions that Einstein made in his calculations of both special relativity and general relativity were found to be accurate not long after he made them. Special relativity and general relativity spawned new fields of science, as well. Special relativity, as expressed in $E=mc^2$, perfectly explains what occurs when producing nuclear energy. A small amount of mass in hydrogen particles, for example, can create large amounts of energy. Many scholars have also pointed to the fact that Einstein's equation enabled the development of the atomic bomb as it was used by the United States in World War II.

Even the heat within Earth's crust can be explained by Einstein's equation. According to the physicist John Rigden, "When [uranium and thorium in the Earth's crust] decay, some of the mass is lost and a little energy is created, and that keeps the crust warm ... So the temperature of the outer Earth, the crustal matter, is directly related to $E=mc^2$."

But, of course, some of the most important consequences of Einstein's theories were related to our nascent understanding of the universe—and were made more widely applicable by astronomical research during this exciting time of discovery.

Light Bends

In 1911, Einstein predicted, using his theory of general relativity, that the light from other stars would bend as they reached the sun and were affected by its gravity. The problem was that many observational astronomers did not have the mathematical background to be able to understand and apply Einstein's formulas and, of course, Einstein was a mathematician and not an astronomer. However, a British astrophysicist named Arthur Eddington had the background to understand general relativity and became one of Einstein's biggest proponents in England. In 1919, Eddington observed and photographed a solar eclipse off the coast of Africa. On Earth, the sun would be blocked by the moon just at the time it was passing by a group of bright stars called the Hyades. Eddington predicted that the light from the Hyades would be bent by the sun's gravity and would be observable due to the blocked light during the eclipse. After taking and analyzing the photos, Eddington declared that his photos proved

Einstein's prediction that light from other stars would be bent by the sun's gravitation. This was an important moment in confirming the general theory of relativity. Headlines around the world trumpeted this information, with the *London Times* declaring: "Revolution in Science/New Theory of the Universe/ Newtonian Ideas Overthrown." Einstein's ideas passed into greater acceptance, although scientists later showed that this evidence was "far from conclusive."

This is called an ***experimentum crucius***, when observations are used to prove or disprove theoretical calculations. For several years after Einstein developed his theories of relativity, few of these experiments were conducted because many scientists in the applied sciences did not have the knowledge base to understand Einstein's more abstract theories. However, gradually his theory was applied to observable science. In 1915, calculations using general relativity finally predicted Mercury's previously unpredictable orbit around the sun. In fact, it was Mercury's strange orbit that had first caught Einstein's imagination and made him question the predictions of Newtonian gravity in the first place.

Black Holes and Wormholes

But Einstein also predicted the existence of things that seemed too strange to be true: **black holes** and **wormholes**. According to Einstein, black holes would be created when a massive star burned out and its own gravitational forces would cause it to shrink into itself. If the star was large enough, it would shrink to a very small mass with infinite density. According to rules of general relativity, space-time would bend around this collapsed star and light would be sucked into it with no light able to escape. This is why such a collapsed star is called a "black hole"; because no light reflects off of it, it is completely invisible both to the human eye and to photography. However, scientists have

The total solar eclipse in 1919 enabled Arthur Eddington to confirm Einstein's general theory of relativity.

detected many black holes since Einstein's time by using X-rays to detect the enormous amount of heat, or energy, it gives off (of course, according to $E=mc^2$, the mass the massive star loses must be converted to energy). Today, many astronomers believe that most galaxies contain very large, or supermassive, black holes at their center. There are many correlations between the age of a galaxy, its size, and the size or amount of black holes in it. Although this relationship is not completely understood today, many scientists believe that black holes are an integral part of the evolution of galaxies.

Just as general relativity was able to predict black holes so, too, did it predict the existence of strange cosmic objects

This supermassive black hole in the Centaurus A galaxy ejects jets of plasma at roughly one-half the speed of light, which shows the extent of its power.

called wormholes. Einstein originally theorized wormholes as "Einstein-Rosen bridges" in 1935 with Nathan Rosen. They saw wormholes as a consequence of the bending of space-time in general relativity. Wormholes are, in some ways, the theoretical reverse of black holes. Rather than drawing all matter and energy in, wormholes "eject" matter and energy outward. Some scientists have speculated that they could exist on the "other side" of a black hole, possibly in the same or even a different universe. Wormholes could be shortcuts between distant points in both space and space-time, as posited by the well-known physicist Stephen Hawking, which would allow energy traveling within wormholes to cover both great distances as well as to travel between moments in time! (This, however, is believed by many scientists to be impossible because of the instability of wormholes as well as the possibility of **feedback loops**, which would deposit matter or energy in one place to infinite levels until the wormhole would be destroyed.)

The COSMOLOGICAL CONSTANT

Using the formulas from general relativity, Einstein saw that it predicted that the universe would either expand or contract. This was previous to Hubble's observations and calculations that proved that the universe was expanding. At the time that Einstein was working on general relativity, around 1915, he did not believe that it was possible for the universe to be expanding. So he went back to his calculations to understand how he could come up with a cosmological constant, positing that the universe was in a constant state.

Later, of course, Einstein would regret making this change to his theory because he understood that his initial theory was, in fact, correct. In 1917, he introduced the **cosmological constant** to his equations, which was signified by the mathematical letter lambda. According to Einstein, this cosmological constant acted as "anti-gravity" and prevented the universe from contracting in on itself into one enormous black hole. Alexander Friedmann later solved this problem of why the universe hadn't yet collapsed on itself with his idea of an original explosive event that caused the universe to continue to expand billions of years later. This, of course, would be the big bang theory. According to Friedmann, if there was enough mass the universe would begin to contract. If, however, there was too little mass to force this reversal, the universe would expand forever. A balanced amount of mass in the universe, according to Friedmann, would cause the universe to slow its expansion until it stopped.

QUANTUM THEORY

Scientists began experimenting with quantum theory, otherwise known as quantum mechanics, long before Albert Einstein came along. Quantum mechanics is the general theory that describes how very small objects, atoms and subatomic particles, interact with one another. Quantum mechanics, as we know it today, evolved from the work of a German physicist named Max Planck around the turn of the twentieth century. However, it was later substantially revised by Albert Einstein.

In 1894, Planck attempted to understand a scientific problem that no one had been able to solve. For decades, scientists had tried to understand why blackbody surfaces, a name used to describe certain surfaces that absorb all light and do not reflect any, did not act according to classical, Newtonian physics. A scientist named Gustav Kirchhoff previously stated the question: "How does the intensity of the electromagnetic radiation emitted by a black body depend on the frequency of the radiation and the temperature of the body?"

In 1900, during an experiment with heated objects giving off so-called **blackbody radiation**, Planck discovered that some colors were not being emitted. Previously, scientists believed that colors were emitted in waves. However, Planck's experiment showed that colors are actually emitted as small packets of energy called **quanta**. Today, we call these photons, thanks to the contributions of Albert Einstein in 1905. Einstein also theorized that particles of light, or photons, are emitted when they collide with other subatomic particles, and that light acts as both a wave and a particle (called wave-particle duality). Just as Einstein realized that large-bodied objects did not always follow Newtonian physics, so, too, did he understand following Planck's experiment that atomic and subatomic particles acted differently than expected. Over the next several decades, scientists would begin to discover atomic particles and how they interacted.

Quantum Mechanic's "Imprecision"

Quantum mechanics was another way of revising classic Newtonian physics to describe the way very small objects interact with one another. With regular-sized objects, forces act on one another according to somewhat predictable ways—for example, Newton's explanation of how and why the apple accelerated while it fell from the tree due to the force of gravity. Very small objects, like atomic particles, however, do not always act in these predictable ways. Rather, it is easier for scientists to estimate what will happen to very small particles that are acted on by a force according to probability. They can say there is a certain chance that this will happen and another chance that something else will happen.

This is called the **uncertainty principle**, and it was first theorized by a theoretical physicist named Werner Heisenberg. According to Heisenberg's uncertainty principle (called *Ungenauigkeit*, or "imprecision," in German), certain variables of small particles, such as speed, acceleration, and location, cannot be known together. Thus, if a scientist knows that a certain atomic particle is traveling at a precise speed and with a certain acceleration, that scientist will not be able to know the exact location of the particle. Of course, this flies in the face of Newtonian physics, which states that if you know the starting point, the speed, and the acceleration of an object (as with the earlier partygoers example), you can know with reasonably certainty where that object will end up after a certain amount of time. The reason why there is this necessary uncertainty with very small atomic particles is because, as Einstein discovered, they can act as waves, too. With larger amounts of matter, the uncertainty present in the system is less well known. However, with smaller amounts of matter, it is more readily visible to the scientific eye. This is why the uncertainty principle applies to all matter in our universe but is usually described only in regard to atomic particles in quantum theory. Newtonian, or classical, physics approximates what will happen when forces act on large amounts of matter; however, it fails to approximate what will occur with small amounts of matter.

As quantum mechanics and the science involving atomic particles continued to develop, most notably through the work of physicist Niels Bohr, Einstein grew increasingly uncomfortable with the direction it was taking. He felt that any statistical uncertainty in regard to subatomic and atomic particles must reflect our own lack of knowledge and not describe the physical rules of the system itself.

The following example illustrates Einstein's problem with the accepted thought in quantum mechanics at the time:

> If an atom has a probability of one half of **radioactive decay** over an hour, then all that really means is that its wave function describes an ensemble of many different atomic systems, half of which decay in an hour. Whether one particular atom in the ensemble will decay in one hour is definitely determinable. However, we will not be able to discern it if all we know is the quantum wave associated with it. Whether it decays or not depends upon properties of that system that have been smoothed away by the quantum wave and thus are unknown to us. It is our ignorance of these smoothed away properties that makes a probabilistic assertion the best we can do.

Thus, Einstein believed that this complex system of interrelating functions governed quantum mechanics, instead of the popular opinion that it was just statistical uncertainty. If we could better understand these processes, according to Einstein, we would be better able to predict what would happen to the system next. This led Einstein to make his famous declaration that "[q]uantum mechanics is very worthy of regard. But an inner voice tells me that this is not yet the right track. The theory yields much, but it hardly brings us closer to the Old One's secrets. I, in any case, am convinced that *He* does not play dice."

The DOUBLE-SLIT EXPERIMENT

There is one famous experiment that shows the strange behavior of atomic and subatomic particles and Einstein's difficulty in unifying quantum mechanics and general relativity. The double-slit experiment illustrates particle-wave duality and shows the strange behavior that atomic particles exhibit in quantum theory. Everyone knows that if you have a hole, here called a slit, in a wall and shine a light through that hole onto another surface, or a screen, that you will have a single shape of light projected onto this screen. However, if you have two holes that are close together, you will not observe two different projections of light onto the screen. Rather, you will see bands of light with alternating brightnesses. The brightest band of light will be in the center of the projection. According to astronomer Laurance R. Doyle,

> This shows that light is a wave since such a pattern results from the interference of the waves coming from slit one (which we shall call "A") with the waves coming from slit two "which we shall call "B"). When peaks of waves from light source A meet peaks from light source B, they add and the bright lines are produced. Not far to the left and right of this brightness peak, however, peaks from A meet troughs from B (because the crests of the light waves are no longer aligned) and a dark line is produced.

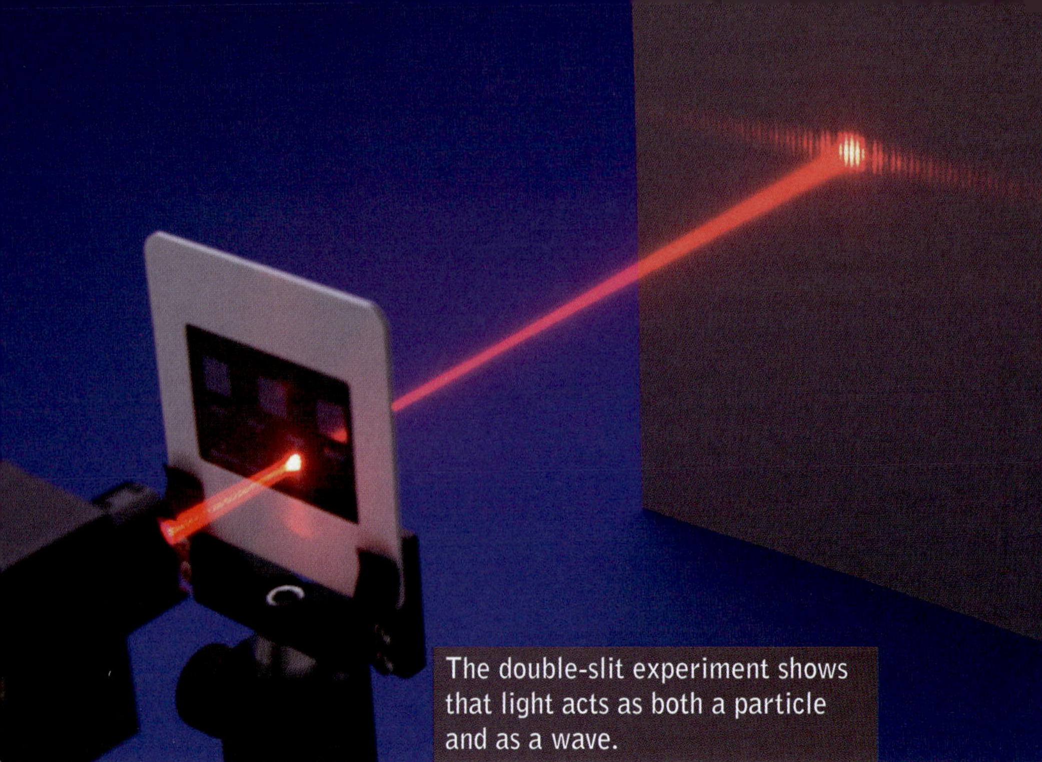
The double-slit experiment shows that light acts as both a particle and as a wave.

Scientists have known about this problem with the double-slit experiment since the nineteenth century. How and why does light act as a particle in some circumstances and as a wave in others? This is what Planck hoped to clarify with his blackbody experiment, and he discovered that light was delivered in packets of particles, called quanta, allowing it to act as both a particle and a wave.

But there is another issue with the double-slit experiment. If you send only one photon through these two slits that are close to one another, the same pattern of bright and dark bands of light is produced on the screen. If only one particle of light is sent through this system, why would it still act as a wave?

According to Doyle,

> The answer is that each individual photon must…have gone through both slits! This, the simplest of quantum weirdness experiments, has been the basis of many of the unintuitive interpretations of quantum physics. We

> can see, perhaps, how physicists might conclude, for example, that a particle of light is not a particle unit until it is measured at the screen. It turns out that the particle of light is rather a wave before it is measured. But it is not a wave…of matter but, rather, it turns out that it is apparently a wave of probability. That is, the elementary particles making up the trees, people, and planets—what we see around us—are apparently just distributions of likelihood until they are measured (that is, measured or observed).

This reflects what we call Heisenberg's uncertainty principle. In other words, on an atomic level, matter does not exist as we imagine it to exist until it is observable. Before it is observable, all that exists of matter is its probability of existing!

A scientist named Richard Feynman further experimented with this problem. The conclusion he reached is even more perplexing. If you put a detector at either one of the slits, then the strange "interference pattern" does not occur. Even the possibility of knowing which path a photon takes removes the interference pattern. However, if it is unknowable and unobservable, then the interference pattern will occur. Doyle states: "This is the most fundamental concept in quantum physics—knowable and unknowable."

Why is this important to astronomy? Because if the possibilities for every atomic particle are endless until observation, then there are infinite number of paths that our universe could follow until one possibility is measured. This was the view that quantum mechanics gave to astronomy until a colleague of Einstein's, John Wheeler, came up with another idea. Called the "participatory universe," Wheeler's theory is that the universe actively participates in all of these possibilities. Wheeler also called this "it from bit" and described it thus:

> It from bit. Otherwise put, every "it"—every particle, every field of force, even the space-time continuum itself—derives its function, its meaning, its very existence entirely—even if in some contexts indirectly—from the apparatus-elicited answers to yes-or-no questions, binary choices, bits. "It from bit" symbolizes the idea that every item of the physical world has at bottom—a very deep bottom, in most instances—an immaterial source and explanation; that which we call reality arises in the last analysis from the posing of yes-or-no questions and the registering of equipment-evoked responses; in short, that all things physical are information-theoretic in origin and that this is a participatory universe.

Put very simply, Wheeler's explanation means that consciousness does not derive from matter, but rather that matter derives from consciousness. An exploration of the theoretical possibilities of both general relativity and quantum mechanics brings us to ask large questions about our universe—and our role in it.

Jan Hendrik Oort

Born in the Netherlands in 1900, Jan Oort would revolutionize the field of radio astronomy—and postulate the existence of dark matter long before other astronomers, such as Fritz Zwicky and Vera Rubin, showed calculations proving its existence.

Oort is known for many discoveries in astronomy, and he is often named as one of the greatest astronomers of the twentieth century. He was the first to declare that the sun was not the center of the Milky Way galaxy and that it rotated in space. While studying the shape of the Milky Way galaxy in 1932, he first postulated that something like dark matter had to account for its missing mass based on motions of stars in the galaxy. Later, he developed many important insights about comets, including that they must come from a particular place in our solar system, which is now named the Oort cloud. In addition to the Oort cloud, the Oort constants and an asteroid, 1691 Oort, were all named after him.

Albert Einstein, Edwin Hubble (with his ever-present pipe), and astronomer Walter Adams look through a telescope.

CHAPTER 3

The Major Players in the Discovery of Dark Matter and Dark Energy

Astronomy, like many other sciences, is not a field in which individual women and men typically make important discoveries by themselves. Rather, astronomical work often requires many years of intense study that offers an important, yet often small, contribution that adds to scientists' previous and future discoveries. The pursuit of scientific breakthroughs is perhaps best represented by a sand castle: the first grain of sand is just as important to the structure as the last grain of sand, but the first grains are often invisible until they form enough of a structure to stand out. Sometimes beautiful, intricate castles result from millions of grains of sands stacked in just the right way, and sometimes a weakness in the castle means that it all comes tumbling down. But the sand is there, just waiting to be fit in the right place once again to form a new theory that will shake the scientific community.

Of course, scientific thought is not as fragile as a castle made of sand, but oftentimes theories that are thought to be sound for generations tumble in the face of new evidence.

Before Nicolaus Copernicus, most astronomers believed for hundreds—if not thousands—of years that Earth lay at the center of our solar system. Before Einstein, our knowledge of physics depended on classical, Newtonian physics and the physics of our universe remained largely unknown.

Scientific inquiry is the result of the work of many scientists who pool together their knowledge and work on each other's discoveries to arrive at a moment of breakthrough. Many scientists who do important work remain unrecognized while those who "discover" a theory (usually building on previous scientists' work) receive most, and sometimes all, of the credit.

FRITZ ZWICKY and CALTECH

A Bulgarian-born Swiss astronomer named Fritz Zwicky was instrumental in discovering dark matter. Born in 1898, in Varna, Bulgaria, Zwicky always showed a propensity for math and science. He studied at the Swiss Federal Institute of Technology in Zurich, Switzerland, before coming to the United States at the age of twenty-seven on a Rockefeller Foundation grant. Zwicky made his home at the California Institute of Technology (known as Caltech) in Pasadena, California. For astronomers in the 1920s, Pasadena—and Caltech—was the center of astronomical innovation. If you wanted to make more discoveries about the universe, Pasadena was the place to be.

Caltech is a world-famous university for those studying and researching science, and especially astronomy. Many famous astronomers have worked and taught at Caltech, including Robert Millikan, who would become a close associate of Zwicky's, and Walter Baade. Edwin Hubble first determined that our galaxy was not alone in the universe using the Hooker telescope on the top of Mount Wilson, which is located about half an hour away in the neighboring San Gabriel

Mountains. Other astronomers would soon flock to Caltech and Mount Wilson, especially with a $6 million grant given to the university the same year Zwicky arrived there, which would go toward funding a telescope with a mirror that was double the size of Hubble's Hooker telescope. This was to ensure "that Pasadena would remain the astronomical center of the universe for decades to come." Arriving the same year, Zwicky would prove to be an important part of this ground zero for astronomical discoveries.

But, Zwicky wasn't really an astronomer—he was a physicist. Zwicky's specialty wasn't necessarily observing the universe and the matter in it, but in using mathematical calculations to determine and predict the movement of celestial objects due to the laws of physics. This, however, didn't faze the industrious Zwicky. Instead, he determined that he could do both astronomy and physics, and he became Caltech's first astrophysicist.

When Zwicky arrived at Caltech, it wasn't just the area surrounding Pasadena and Mount Wilson that was experiencing a scientific renaissance—it was the world. Einstein had published on his theory of general relativity just over ten years earlier, and physicists were just beginning to look into and experiment with the strange world of quantum mechanics. Zwicky had the background as a physicist to enter into this exciting new domain of **astrophysics**, and he had the unconventional genius to see the universe in a different way than everyone else. "There's no doubt that he had a mind that was quite extraordinary," the former director of Caltech astronomy said about him.

Zwicky's background, his unconventional genius, and the exciting time in physics in which he worked all converged to allow him to make some of the most important astronomical discoveries of our time. In 1934, only several years after the British scientist James Chadwich discovered the neutron,

Zwicky and Walter Baade theorized that the explosions of certain stars would lead to a very compact star, later coined by Zwicky as a "neutron star," made up of an extremely dense neutron-packed core. He also named the explosion that would lead to these neutron stars: **supernova**.

Zwicky was also one of the first scientists to explore the consequences of Einstein's general theory of relativity. If, as Einstein postulated, a star's gravity could bend the light of a more distant object around it, then Zwicky stated that this gravitational force would be much larger—and easier to observe—when looking at larger objects, such as galaxies. One of Zwicky's greatest discoveries wouldn't actually be discovered for nearly forty years. After observing galaxies that moved at speeds that would defy the laws of gravity (and general relativity), Zwicky proposed something he called *Dunkle Materie*, which would be translated as "dark matter."

Later, Zwicky's unending curiosity would lead him to other discoveries: In the 1940s, after being appointed professor at Caltech, he was appointed director of research for Aerojet Engineering. While there, Zwicky invented and patented more than fifty jet engines for jet-assisted takeoff, which would allow airplanes to lift off the ground faster on a short runway.

Also during this time, Zwicky stated that he no longer thought that astronomers should be "passive observers" of space and advocated for so-called "experimental astronomy." According to Richard Panek:

> "Shoot the moon," [Zwicky] counseled, and watch the effects through a telescope on Earth. Shoot the atmosphere of Venus—and Mars, too. And not just shoot. Rearrange. Use nuclear energy to flatten mountains on the moon and to alter the orbits of planets. Nudge Mars closer to the sun and see if it becomes habitable. Nudge the sun itself. Send it and all its gravitationally bound bodies, including Earth,

> toward a star with habitable planets so we might one day colonize other solar systems.

Today, Zwicky and his important discoveries are often passed over. A recent article about him, titled, "The Father of Dark Matter Still Gets No Respect," explores how his reputation as a "curmudgeon" often precedes his reputation as one of the most important astrophysicists of all time. Apparently, during his time at Caltech, Zwicky had the reputation of being difficult to work with. Often his difficult personality gets more attention than his important scientific discoveries. According to his youngest daughter,

> Fritz Zwicky revealed a genesis of astounding cosmological achievements that still illuminate the scientific world. He was a scientific prophet and the sacrificial lamb for the provincial judgment of his colleagues. His [intellect was so strong and his scientific predictions so accurate] that the standard mind only could falter in their presence.

Whatever his personal conflicts with colleagues, Zwicky was, indeed, a brilliant man and a prescient thinker. Often, scientific innovation—and the greatest discoveries in astronomy and physics—are the result not just of intelligence, but creativity. For example, Einstein's theory of relativity did not come about from very complex mathematical calculations but from a fresh and innovative way of observing our universe. For Zwicky, too, the breadth of his innovation came from his unique ability to see the universe and anticipate new answers to age-old questions. Possibly his most important—and most far-out—conclusion was the existence of a strange substance called "black matter." Zwicky died in 1974, just several years before evidence of dark matter started popping up. While

Zwicky didn't see the direction his discovery would take, the man who once called himself the most important physicist since Einstein wouldn't be surprised at the important place it would take in the history of astronomy.

VERA RUBIN

Vera Rubin was born to Philip and Rose Cooper on July 23, 1928, in Philadelphia, Pennsylvania. Her father was an electrical engineer, and her mother worked for Bell Telephone Company. Her father, Philip, was interested in astronomy as a hobby and encouraged Vera's interest in it as well. After school, he would take her to amateur astronomer meetings in Washington, D.C., where the Cooper family moved when Vera was still a young girl. Together, daughter and father worked on building a telescope when she was just fourteen.

But astronomy was not an easy domain for women to gain access to during the middle of the twentieth century. In fact, many colleges would not even accept women students into their science and astronomy programs. Upon graduating from high school, however, she was determined to get a degree in astronomy and to pursue her passion, despite the sexism that she encountered.

She spent four years studying astronomy at Vassar College, which was, at that time, a women's only college in New York. (Vassar College began accepting male students in 1969 and is now co-ed.) After graduating as the sole astronomy major at Vassar in 1951, she dreamed of attending Princeton University for graduate school. She sent away for the Princeton astronomy graduate program but never received anything back in the mail. Upon inquiring, she was told that Princeton University would not accept female graduate students.

She did not let this dissuade her. She applied to the physics graduate program at Cornell University in Ithaca, New York, and was accepted. While there, she studied under many famous

Vera Rubin discovered the strongest evidence for the existence of dark matter.

physicists, including Philip Morrison, Richard Feynman, and Hans Bethe. She also met and married Robert Rubin, who was a graduate student in chemistry. Rubin received her master's degree from Cornell in 1951 after writing her thesis on the "sideways" motion of certain galaxies she observed. She stated that galaxies didn't move straight outward during the expansion of the universe, but that they rotated around an unknown center as they moved outward. This thesis proved to be too controversial for publication and was rejected by many well-known academic journals. However, it is also likely that Rubin's research was rejected due to the simple fact that she was a woman in a male-dominated field.

Next, Rubin headed back home to Washington, D.C., where she would pursue her doctorate in astronomy at Georgetown University. Her advisor was none other than George Gamow, a famous cosmologist who was one of the earliest advocates of the big bang theory. Gamow requested to advise Rubin when he heard about her master's dissertation because he, too, thought that galaxies might be rotating instead of just moving in straight paths. Rubin continued her doctorate work while taking care of her children, a son born in 1950 and a daughter born in 1952. The Rubins would have two more sons in 1956 and 1960.

Rubin received her doctorate in 1954 for her dissertation on how galaxies were not evenly distributed across the sky, but rather were often distributed in groups. This was some of the earliest work done on **galaxy clusters** and their distribution, and it would receive little attention by the larger scientific community until the 1970s. One of Rubin's main conclusions from her dissertation is that the universe is not in stasis but is rather in a constant state of chaos.

Rubin was subsequently hired as a professor at Georgetown, where she remained for several years. In 1963, Rubin became interested in observational astronomy. She applied to use the Palomar Observatory, outside of San

Vera Rubin was the first female astronomer to be granted access to the Palomar telescope.

Diego, California, for her research. This would prove to be an important moment for both Rubin and for women in astronomy: When she was granted access, Rubin became the first woman ever allowed to use the Palomar telescope. This shows how little access female astronomers had to the instruments that were essential to their research at this time.

Then, in 1965, Rubin began working at the Carnegie Institute, also in Washington, D.C. It was here that she would make some of her biggest discoveries and where she would stay for the remainder of her career. In the 1970s, Rubin decided that she wanted to go back to study the sideways motion she had detected in certain galaxies as a graduate student. Collaborating with an astronomer named W. Kent Ford, Rubin found more evidence of this strange motion in galaxies that the scientific community refused to accept. In 1976, this was declared the Rubin-Ford effect. It is the name given to the strange way in which spiral galaxies move, which defies previous mathematical modeling. According to mathematical calculations, stars at the edge of these galaxies should move more slowly than stars that are closer to the center. This is because the force of gravity is much stronger where the majority of its mass is at the center of the galaxy. Thus, astronomers expected stars in the center to move fastest. However, according to the Rubin-Ford effect, all of the stars in the observed galaxies moved at a constant rate. This was incredibly surprising and would lead her to a much larger discovery: dark matter.

Rubin went on to earn numerous awards and accolades for her work. She was awarded four honorary doctorates, the prestigious Presidential National Medal of Science in 1993, and many other awards. In 1981, Rubin became the second woman in astronomy to be elected to the National Academy of Sciences. Her four children have all gone on to earn Ph.D.s themselves in math and science, and her daughter, Judith Young, became a well-known astronomer for her own work with galaxies before her death in 2014. Today, in her late eighties, Rubin is still active in astronomy.

Rubin is known not just for her work with galaxies, but for her dedication to other women in astronomy. For years she has traveled around the United States and spoken to students about astronomy and the importance of women in the field. She has also mentored many young astronomers. As she has said, "It is well known … that I am available twenty-four hours a day to women astronomers."

Although divided by nearly thirty years, Zwicky's and Rubin's work would form the basis of cosmologists' new inquiry into the universe. Zwicky and Rubin, who themselves built on the work of many scientists before them—and especially, on the theories developed by Albert Einstein—would help future astronomers better understand our universe. Together, Zwicky and Rubin would postulate and then prove the existence of something called dark matter in our universe, which would, in turn, lead to the discovery of dark energy. Suddenly, cosmologists would be faced with the fact that our universe is not relatively empty and is, in fact, being propelled outward at ever increasing speeds.

This doesn't mean, however, that the questions that Zwicky and Rubin put forth with their research have been answered. It is, in fact, quite the contrary. Today, due to our knowledge of the existence of dark matter and dark energy, astronomers have more questions than ever before. Nothing has reenergized astronomers' quest for understanding our universe more than these discoveries.

And questions provide fertile ground for new discoveries, after all.

SAUL PERLMUTTER, ADAM G. RIESS, and BRIAN SCHMIDT

In 2011, three men who lived and worked thousands of miles away from one another won the Noble Prize in Physics for "the discovery of the accelerating expansion of the Universe through observations of distant supernovae."

Although they worked nearly several generations after Rubin and Zwicky, they would yet again build on these other astronomers' discoveries into dark matter. The discovery that our universe is picking up speed as it continues to expand, which won these men the prestigious Nobel Prize, surprised the scientists themselves at first. Even more surprising was the reason behind this acceleration: so-called dark energy. According to the Nobel Prize committee, Perlmutter, Riess, and Schmidt's discovery has "[unveiled] a Universe that to a large extent is unknown to science. And [which makes] everything ... possible again."

Saul Perlmutter was born in 1959 in Champaign-Urbana, Illinois. He spent his childhood in Philadelphia and went to college at Harvard University, where he graduated with an AB

Saul Perlmutter, shown here, was awarded the Nobel Prize in Physics in 2011 along with Adam G. Riess and Brian P. Schmidt for their discovery of the accelerating expansion of the universe.

in physics in 1981. After graduating from Harvard, he was accepted in the graduate program in physics at the University of California, Berkeley. His dissertation explored the use of a certain kind of automated telescope, which he would later use to observe distant supernovae.

Later, Perlmutter became a professor at Berkeley and cofounded the Supernova Cosmology Project (SCP) at Lawrence Berkeley National Laboratory with Carl Pennypacker. SCP focused on supernovae, which are the explosions at the last stages of certain massive stars' lives, because they develop according to a particular pattern and

Adam G. Riess currently works as a professor of astrophysics at Johns Hopkins University.

always have almost the same level of brightness. Perlmutter believed that by studying these supernovae, he would be able to analyze how fast the universe was expanding.

The fruit of Perlmutter's many years of observing supernovae and calculating their distances finally came in 1998, when he discovered that the universe is expanding at an increasingly rapid rate. Just two weeks later, a separate team based out of Australia would publish a paper showing similar results. These two independent results would be all the proof needed for the existence of a mysterious quantity known as dark energy, which propels the universe's expansion at a faster and faster rate, and it showed that many bright minds working together can revolutionize our understanding of the universe.

Nobel Prize Winner Professor Brian Schmidt

Nobel Prize–winning astronomer Brian Schmidt moved from the United States to Australia in the 1990s to pursue his research on supernovae. While much of Schmidt's time is spent on researching our universe, he also cultivates grapes from which he makes wine. You can follow Schmidt on Twitter—and his work in both astronomy and wine—through the hashtag #CosmicPinot.

According to ABC Melbourne, "Professor Schmidt sees the Nobel physics award as something that is a positive for Australian science in general and hopes his example will inspire others to give young people a chance in their chosen fields." Schmidt said:

> The work I've done really was made possible by the way Australia does science; I think hopefully it shows the opportunity we have here in Australia to do great work—so I hope it's an inspiration—but I also think it's a celebration of the science that has been done here in Australia by astronomy, and by physics as a whole.

Professor Schmidt has been vocal about the need for governmental funding in Australia for young scientists. He states that funding he received from the Australian National University (ANU) was essential to his Nobel Prize–winning research and that other scientists should be given the opportunity to concentrate on research that could change the course of astronomy and physics, as well. According to ABC Melbourne, the financial award that he received from ANU "should be used as a starting point to evaluate how science can be better supported and funded in the future."

Brian P. Schmidt is not just a Nobel Prize–winning astrophysicist, but also a winemaker and vineyard owner.

The Coma cluster of galaxies, photographed by Fritz Zwicky, allowed him to postulate the existence of dark matter.

CHAPTER 4

The Discovery of Dark Matter

Fritz Zwicky was a Swiss astronomer who spent most of his professional life at California Institute of Technology. In addition to being an observational astronomer, he also performed all of his own mathematical calculations. This is rare, as cosmologists normally outsource specialized mathematical work. But Zwicky's unique ability as one of the country's earliest astrophysicists would help him to revolutionize astronomical study.

The DISCOVERY of *DUNKLE MATERIE*

In the early 1930s, Zwicky convinced Caltech to build an advanced 18-inch (45.72 cm) telescope so he could observe distant galaxies. The large diameter of this telescope would be especially useful, as Zwicky wanted to capture multiple galaxies—all located in the Coma cluster of galaxies—in a single photograph.

Using pictures from this telescope and mathematical calculations, including the application of the Doppler shift, he discovered that the light emitted from a cluster of galaxies was much dimmer than it should have been—by a factor of one hundred. The mass from these galaxies was calculated as being incredibly large, so then why would it not emit as much light as Zwicky expected? Even more troublesome, using a mathematical calculation called the **virial theorem**, Zwicky determined that the galaxies were moving too fast for the amount of mass in the system. He wrote:

> In order to receive an average Doppler effect of 1000 km/s or more, which is what we have observed, the average density in the COMA system would have to be at least 400 times greater than that of visible matter. If this can be shown to be the case, then it would have the surprising result that dark matter is present in the Universe in far greater density than visible matter.

Zwicky theorized that there had to be a lot of mass within these galaxies that was not observable and did not give off light—he called this hypothetical mass *Dunkle Materie*, or "dark matter." To many of Zwicky's colleagues, this proposal seemed laughable. How could the amount of invisible matter in our universe be larger than the amount of visible matter? Space was an empty vacuum, and Zwicky's theory flew in the face of common-sense knowledge in the field of astronomy. No one took him seriously. But Zwicky persisted.

In 1937, an undeterred and persistent Zwicky thought of another way in which he could show that dark matter actually existed. If he could find a very large galaxy that was directly between Earth and another, smaller galaxy, he could use Einstein's theory of relativity to prove the existence of dark matter. This is called gravitational lensing, when the mass from a large galaxy actually bends the space around it, which in turn distorts the image of the background galaxy. Using Einstein's calculations, Zwicky predicted that astronomers would be able to use measurements of the distortion of the background galaxy to calculate the mass in the closer galaxy. If this mass was determined to be much larger than was calculated through other, more conventional ways of calculating mass (such as, for example, using luminosity, which can obviously only be used to calculate visible matter), then it would be further proof that dark matter existed.

In addition to this, Zwicky proposed that gravitational lensing could be used to further test Einstein's theory of relativity and to discover much more distant galaxies than could normally be detected.

Unfortunately, Fritz Zwicky was never able to use gravitational lensing to prove the existence of dark matter. However, gravitational lensing has become an important technique by astronomers to discover more distant celestial objects, as well as to study the possible dimensions of the universe itself. And, in time, Zwicky would be vindicated: Indeed, dark matter was proved to exist just several years after his death, and it has become one of the most important astronomical discoveries in the past century. Although Zwicky based his calculations on the accepted Hubble constant of the time, which was later determined to be about seven times too large, his results have now been determined to be generally accurate.

It would take forty more years for Zwicky's hypothesis to be proved correct.

PROOF of DARK MATTER

Vera Rubin wanted to be an astronomer from when she was a little girl. As she grew older, she knew that this would be her career. This female astronomer in a field dominated by men at the time would go on to make one of the greatest astronomical discoveries ever.

Using a device called a spectrometer, which measures the properties of light that filters through it, she and a fellow astronomer named Kent Ford began studying the light that faraway stars emanated from different spiral galaxies in 1978. Like the astronomer Vesto Slipher had previously done, Rubin and Ford hoped to use the spectrometer to calculate the

Doppler shifts of these galaxies. They hoped that they could further calculate the speed of stars in these galaxies using calculations derived from this instrument. They imagined that they would be able to make this calculation because the position of stars in galaxies would affect their velocity. Stars in the center of a galaxy should move faster than those at the outskirts of that galaxy because most of the mass and density would be located at the center, which would provide additional force the closer a star was to its center.

They were surprised to calculate that this was not the case at all. Instead, according to their calculations, stars at the center of the spiral galaxies that they studied were moving just as fast as those that were on the edge of those galaxies. At first, Rubin and Ford thought that they must have made a mistake somewhere. What they were observing just wasn't possible. The gravitational force on stars at the center of galaxies would be much stronger than on stars farther out in less-dense areas. This gravitational force would increase the speeds of stars closer to the center.

Vera Rubin did not give up on her calculations, however. She and Ford went back and calculated how much invisible mass would be necessary for the stars on the outskirts of certain galaxies to move just as quickly as the stars nearer the center. According to these calculations, galaxies would have to contain 90 percent of this "dark," or invisible, mass and only 10 percent of mass that was visible and known to astronomers! Rubin and Ford continued to observe and calculate other spiral galaxies, and their results were always the same. Now, it seemed to Rubin that she hadn't made a mistake or just found a galaxy that operated in an abnormal way—every single galaxy that she found would need to contain much more mass than was visible in order for her calculations to work.

Suddenly, Rubin remembered an exercise she had done in graduate school. For this class assignment, she had to use calculations Fritz Zwicky had made about the mass and velocities of certain cluster galaxies. She remembered an important point:

Zwicky had mentioned that there must be some "missing mass" from these cluster galaxies that kept them together despite their rapid movement. Could this be the missing mass that Zwicky had postulated more than forty years earlier? The scientific community had laughed at Zwicky's proposal, and his theory had been largely forgotten. But Rubin's calculations, along with her knowledge of Zwicky's unaccepted theory, made her think that she had proof that this so-called "missing matter," otherwise known as dark matter, could actually exist.

Vera Rubin showed her observations and calculations to other scientists and published her findings. There was no other explanation for it. There had to be dark matter in the universe. According to Rubin's calculations, if dark matter accounted for 90 percent of all matter, then astronomers had spent the entire history of mankind studying only 10 percent of our universe!

Rubin explains it like this:

> Imagine, for a moment, that one night you awaken abruptly from a dream. Coming to consciousness, blinking your eyes against the blackness, you find that, inexplicably, you are standing alone in a vast, pitch-black cavern. Befuddled by this predicament, you wonder: Where am I? What is this space? What are its dimensions?
>
> Groping in the darkness, you stumble upon a book of damp matches. You strike one; it quickly flares, then fizzles out. Again, you try; again, a flash and fizzle. But in that moment, you realize that you can glimpse a bit of your surroundings. The next match strike lets you sense faint walls far away. Another flare reveals a strange shadow, suggesting the presence of a big object. Yet another suggests you are moving—or, instead, the room is moving relative to you. With each momentary flare, a bit more is learned.

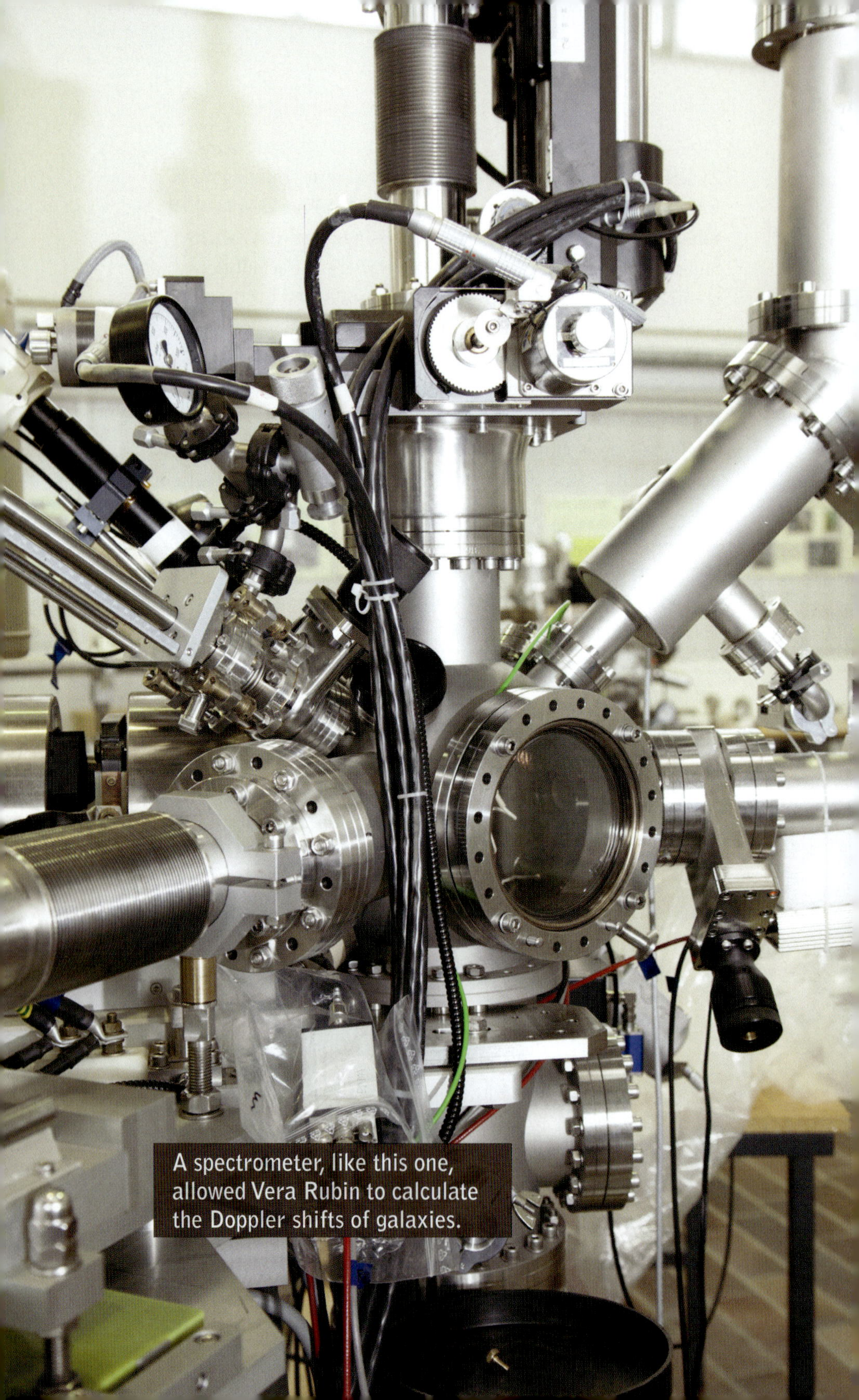

A spectrometer, like this one, allowed Vera Rubin to calculate the Doppler shifts of galaxies.

Rubin says that this explains our search to understand our universe. With each flicker of the match, scientists are able to see a glimpse of something more—but just a brief glimpse. Gradually, hundreds and thousands of these tiny glimpses into the darkness of space build up to create a larger picture. But, as Rubin states, "… what we do discern about [objects in space] tells us that there is much more that we cannot yet see."

The discovery of dark matter has been so profound and important to astronomers because it has been a reminder that, despite all of our knowledge, we still know only a fraction about our universe. But, as Rubin states, we must do better—and we must continue our search to know more.

Since Rubin's discovery, many scientists have attempted to answer the question "What is dark matter?" While astronomers have come closer to answering this question, it still remains one of the most intriguing—and important—mysteries in our universe today. Vera Rubin continued to work with galaxies and observed other unusual behavior that was most likely caused by dark matter. However, her biggest breakthrough was still this early discovery of dark matter. She has since said, "We have peered into a new world and have seen that it is more mysterious and more complex than we had imagined. Still more mysteries of the universe remain hidden. Their discovery awaits the adventurous scientists of the future. I like it this way."

And it's true: Rubin's greatest contribution has not been to unravel a mystery, but rather to present the universe as more complex than we could ever have imagined. This has inspired countless other astronomers to continue her search into dark matter—and other great mysteries of our universe.

The PROOF PILES UP

In the early 1970s, just after Rubin and Ford's discovery, another team of astronomers would find proof of dark matter. Like Rubin and Ford, James Peebles and Jeremiah Ostriker studied distant galaxies to see how they behaved. They mapped a group of stars in a galaxy, all of which were rotating around a central point. These scientists were able to do this experiment on a computer—an important piece of technology that Zwicky was not able to use in his experiments.

Using computer technology, Peebles and Ostriker were able to simulate the gravitational force between these objects and predict how fast they would move during a certain period of time. This simulation showed them something strange: using the mass of the stars to chart out rotation periods, in the time it would take a star to orbit a center point, which could be approximately fifty million years, that galaxy would have already collapsed due to gravitational forces. This was odd because the galaxies that Peebles and Ostriker were observing didn't look like dense, collapsed galaxies but fanned out in spiral patterns or took the shape of ellipses. Why were these galaxies not collapsing into themselves?

The answer, of course, could only be one thing: extra mass in these galaxies that allowed them to form and retain their particular shapes. Using the computer simulation, they found that if they added ten times the mass to the galaxy model, it would keep the same shape they observed in the real galaxy. This, too, became solid data that proved that dark matter must exist in these galaxies—and that the amount of dark matter would be approximately ten times the amount of visible matter in a galaxy.

Since then, many scientists have observed proof of the existence of dark matter in distant galaxies. More recently, astronomers have observed clouds of hot gas in galaxies that would have dispersed long ago if not for the gravitational pull exerted by dark matter. Today, it seems like dark matter is an integral part of our universe.

What started as a theory in the 1930s began to show up in evidence in the 1960s and 1970s. By the 1980s and 1990s, more astronomers accepted the evidence of dark matter and began to conduct experiments to learn more about its mysterious composition. This is the way science works: slowly building upon itself, through the work of many scientists, over sometimes half a century or more.

Since the early discovery of what scientists believed was "dark matter," we have come to better know and understand our universe—all while remaining, in some ways, in the "dark."

For example, cosmologists discovered, while learning more about dark matter, that it was not only essential in causing the form of galaxies as we see them today, but in actually constructing our universe as we know it. If not for the gravity caused by dark matter, early matter would not have been drawn together in clusters—and galaxies would never have been born. That means that the Milky Way wouldn't be here today, nor the planet Earth—and, certainly, not us. Dark matter is an essential—albeit invisible—part of why we are able to ask these questions in the first place.

WHAT IS DARK MATTER?

Now that scientists understood that dark matter exists—and that it forms an essential part of our universe—they sought to understand more about it. There were many aspects of dark matter to which scientists could direct their questions.

First of all, scientists asked, what is dark matter? What particles make it up? This is perhaps the hardest question that scientists have been confronted with. That is because, while scientists can observe and calculate the interactions of dark matter, it is harder to state what it is made of. Dark matter is most likely made up of particles that scientists have yet to discover.

But there are other questions that scientists have pursued all in the hope of asking the essential question of what dark matter is. Over the past forty years, scientists have been posing the following questions in relation to dark matter: How does dark matter interact with other matter? How is it distributed in the universe? How was it formed and why? And, importantly, how might our increased study of dark matter teach us about the physical laws that govern our universe?

While we still don't know, exactly, what dark matter is, scientists are answering more of these other questions all the time. Scientists have studied how it interacts and, with the development of incredibly powerful scientific machines, such as CERN's Large Hadron Collider, we understand better how some subatomic particles behave—and what particles we can eliminate as the building blocks of dark matter.

Interactions

A recent studies conducted with NASA's Hubble Space Telescope has provided evidence into how dark matter has evolved and how it interacts with itself. This study, like others conducted before, focuses on clusters of galaxies:

> As two galactic clusters collide, the stars, gas and dark matter interact in different ways. The clouds of gas suffer drag, slow down and often stop, whereas the stars zip past one another, unless they collide—which is rare. On studying what happens to dark matter during these collisions, the researchers realized that, like stars, the colliding clouds of dark matter have little effect on one another.
>
> Thought to be spread evenly throughout each cluster, it seems logical to assume that the clouds of dark matter would have a strong interaction—much like the colliding clouds of gas as the colliding dark matter particles should come into very close proximity. But rather than creating drag, the dark matter clouds slide *through* one another seamlessly.

The Hubble Space Telescope is one of the most important tools astronomers have today to make discoveries about our universe.

Scientists are continuing to explore what happens to dark matter under different kinds of collisions and hope to investigate whether or not dark matter "bounces off" other dark matter and scatters.

Another recent study showed that, when individual galaxies collide, instead of galaxy clusters, dark matter behaves strangely in a different way. In fact, dark matter seems to slow down when it collides with other dark matter, causing a five-thousand-light-year lag.

According to Richard Massey, who conducted the study, "We used to think that dark matter just sits around, minding its own business, except for its gravitational pull. But if dark matter were being slowed down during this collision, it could be the first evidence for rich physics in the dark sector—the hidden Universe all around us."

What this means is that dark matter is interacting with other forces besides gravity, which is causing this slowdown. If this is the case, what is it interacting with?

Formation

Yet another recent study proposes that there was a secondary period of inflation after the big bang that caused the large amount of black matter we calculate to be in the universe today. Previous theories over- or underestimated the amount of dark matter in the universe, but this new theory might get at why we have the exact amount that we observe today.

Physicist Hooman Davoudiasl states,

> In standard cosmology, the exponential expansion of the universe called cosmic inflation began perhaps as early as 10^{-35} seconds after the beginning of time—that's a decimal point followed by 34 zeros before a 1. This explosive expansion of the entirety of space lasted mere fractions of a fraction of a second, eventually leading to a hot universe, followed by a cooling period that has continued until the present day.

It was during this cooling period that lighter elements began to form, which would eventually create all of the mass that is in our universe today. However, according to Davoudiasl, now scientists think that another period of rapid expansion—following the original cosmic inflation—could have occurred before these elements began to form. This would explain the very large amount of dark matter in our universe.

During the initial period of rapid expansion, the universe was incredibly hot, and any dark matter particles would collide and destroy themselves. However, if there was a secondary period of inflation when the universe was much cooler, these

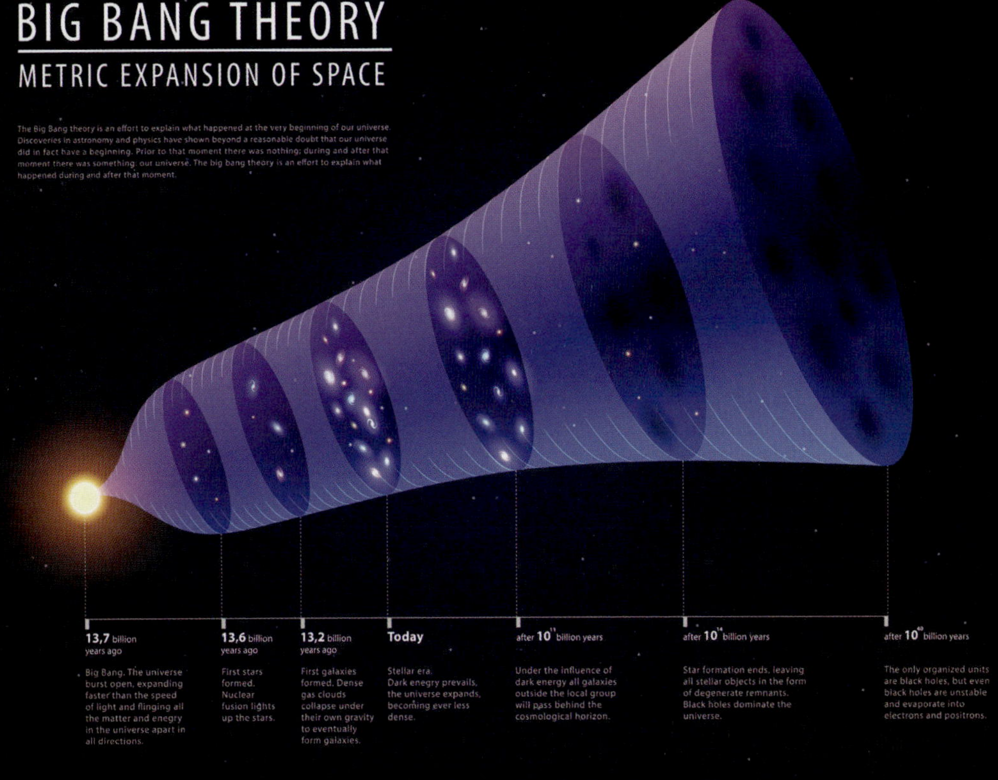

This time line shows important moments that happened during the big bang and what astronomers posit will happen to our universe in the distant future.

dark matter particles would be more spread out and less likely to collide. The dark matter would expand outward before it could be destroyed—thus explaining the amount of dark matter scientists observe today.

According to Davoudiasl, "At this point, the abundance of dark matter is now baked in the cake. Remember, dark matter interacts very weakly … Self-annihilation of dark matter becomes inefficient quite early, and the amount of dark matter particles is frozen." If dark matter could not annihilate itself in these cooler conditions, then the amount of dark matter particles in the universe would stay largely stable from that moment on.

Distribution

Some scientists also began mapping so-called hot and cold spots of the sky using radio telescopes. A difference in temperature variations in cosmic microwave background, discovered by Arno Penzias and Robert Wilson in 1965, can show scientists how dark matter is distributed in the sky.

In the early 1990s, NASA's Cosmic Background Explorer (COBE) and the Wilkinson Microwave Anisotropy Probe (WMAP) created these maps. Evidence from these maps shows that "the universe contained about five times as much dark matter as normal matter when the neutral hydrogen formed. Combined with measurements of supernovae and the clustering of galaxies, this indicates that dark energy comprises 73 percent of the universe, dark matter 23 percent, and normal matter just 4 percent."

Cosmologists have also discovered that, when enough dark matter is formed, "it attracts ordinary matter (mostly hydrogen and helium gas) to form stars that may eventually form a luminous galaxy at the core." This means that the way in which dark matter is formed and evolves can eventually lead to the formation of galaxies themselves. This research is largely due to Vera Rubin's discovery that dark matter often forms the shape of a halo around galaxies, such as our own galaxy the Milky Way. The term "halo" is used to describe how dark matter expands out past areas of galaxies that are dense with baryonic matter.

In 2006, scientists formed a model to show how dark matter gathers together to form the dark halo around the Milky Way. Their research showed how so-called subhalos of dark matter were distributed and then drawn together to form the larger halo around our galaxy. Due to the interaction between dark matter and hydrogen and helium, star clusters were formed.

In 2010, scientists were able to better describe how dark matter is distributed around our galaxy. They described the shape of the Milky Way's dark matter halo as a "squashed beach ball."

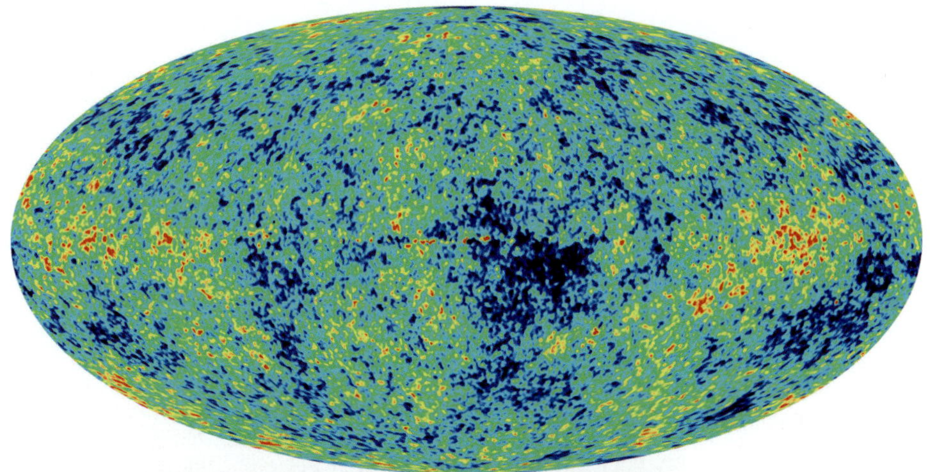

This map made from WMAP data shows the distribution of microwave light after the big bang and is an attempt to map everything—including dark matter—that is present in our universe.

Non-Baryonic Matter and Supersymmetry

But, while astronomers and physicists are having an easier time observing how dark matter interacts and how it is distributed, they still don't know what exactly it is. At first, many scientists believed that dark matter was made up of regular matter, but that it was just non-luminous, or that it did not give off light, making it "dark." Scientists who believed this theory hypothesized that dark matter was made up of something called **massive compact halo objects** (otherwise known as MACHOs), which just means a large grouping of hard-to-see matter.

However, physicists soon discovered that this could not be the case. While a small part of dark matter can be made up of "normal" matter, most of it is not made up of the matter that we consciously interact with on a daily basis.

Normal matter, for example, is the book you are holding, the clothes you are wearing, the floor you are standing on, as well everything that makes up you (this is a simplified example). Physicists call this baryonic matter because it is made up of particles that provide mass and are composed of atoms. But scientists agree that dark matter is made up of non-baryonic matter. The only non-baryonic matter that we know of, which is not made up of **baryons** (a certain kind of subatomic particle), includes neutrinos, dark matter, and black holes.

Today, scientists state that they are looking for particles called WIMPS, or **weakly interacting massive particles**. Most scientists agree that WIMPS are the most likely building blocks of dark matter. WIMPS are as-of-yet undiscovered particles that are probably very large compared to other particles but that don't interact very much with other particles. These particles were created during the big bang and were spread out too quickly to be destroyed.

What is intriguing for scientists about these particles is that they don't fall under the so-called **Standard Model of physics**. The Standard Model of physics was developed in the twentieth century with the advent of particle physics (and is a model within quantum mechanics). This was a period of time when scientists began to study and classify different subatomic particles, and it reached its zenith in the 1970s with the discovery of quarks. What the Standard Model does is predict the existence of particles, as well as their behaviors—and it worked very well for a time, until scientists began to discover the existence of different particles and of the existence of phenomena such as dark matter.

While the Standard Model is an experimentally confirmed model, it still cannot explain gravitation, according to the general theory of relativity. This, of course, relates to the difficulty that scientists have had in completely reconciling quantum mechanics with general relativity—or the world of the very small with the world of the very large. Thus, many scientists believe that the Standard Model does not fully explain how particles interact or the existence of other, undiscovered particles. Another model that might prove more

Subatomic particles revolve around a central nucleus in distinct orbits; the study of these particles falls under the category of particle physics or quantum mechanics.

successful—and what many particle physicists believe is the model we should follow—is called **supersymmetry**.

Supersymmetry is appealing to physicists for one major reason. According to Adam Mann:

> One of the questions keeping physicists up at night is why the four fundamental forces of the universe—gravity, electromagnetism, the weak force, and the strong force—have such differing values. More specifically, why the weak force is approximately 10 quadrillion times as powerful as gravity.

> This is strange because down at the subatomic level, virtual quantum particles are constantly jiggling. This wavering, if left unimpeded should push the energy scale of the weak force away from its observed value. Supersymmetry's popularity derives from its ability to prevent this from happening.

The weak force is a fundamental physical force that allows radioactive particles to decay and only really works at very close distances between particles. Despite its name, this force is stronger than gravity. Supersymmetry explains why this might be possible in a way that the Standard Model doesn't.

Mann continues:

> Like nearly everything having to do with subatomic particles, supersymmetry is weird. Essentially, it says that for every particle we know about—things like electrons, quarks, and neutrinos—there is a corresponding superpartner of higher mass. So the electron would be paired with a particle called a selectron, quarks would have corresponding squarks (much of supersymmetric **nomenclature** simply adds an "s" to the known particles).
>
> If these superpartners exist, they have the property of naturally canceling out the tiny quantum jiggles that would drive the weak force away from its observed range…Some supersymmetry theories have the added advantage of providing ideal candidates for dark matter. Lurking somewhere in all the strange new superpartners might be one that is massive but doesn't interact with light, which is exactly what a dark-matter particle should be.

As professor Matt Strassler states, "[I]f supersymmetry were a symmetry of nature, every type of elementary particle that we know of in nature would have to have partners we have not discovered yet. Since there are over two dozen particles known, that would mean we have a lot of work to do!"

While supersymmetry is an exciting model for particle physics that might provide as-of-yet discovered particles that could reasonably make up the composition of dark matter, it has not yet been proven. With experiments done with **particle colliders** like the Large Hadron Collider, proof of supersymmetry continues to be evasive, and scientists continue to readjust supersymmetric models.

Today, scientists understand that the composition of dark matter cannot fit into standard theories of physics. Dark matter must be made of currently unknown particles that don't fit into or correspond with the Standard Model of physics. But this still leaves a lot of questions to be answered.

These questions are incredibly exciting for cosmologists and particle physicists alike. Many scientists believe that dark matter could help provide the link between quantum mechanics and general relativity—and rewrite our understanding of the universe.

But, dark matter isn't the only exciting and invisible force in our universe that astronomers and physicists are investigating right now. While scientists don't yet know if it is linked with dark matter, dark energy is another exciting discovery that scientists are currently investigating. Like dark matter, the discovery of dark energy has taught astronomers that we still know relatively little about our universe. As Vera Rubin states, we should be excited about what this next stroke of the matchstick will teach us.

The Large Hadron Collider

The Large Hadron Collider (LHC), located near Geneva, Switzerland, is the world's largest particle collider and the biggest machine ever constructed. Built from 1998 to 2008, the LHC is a large underground tunnel that consists of a 17-mile-wide (27-kilometer) ring of magnets, which must be chilled to -456.3 degrees Fahrenheit (-271.3 degrees Celsius). This is colder than outer space!

Within the LHC, streams of particles—with the added push of the magnets—move at nearly the speed of light... until they crash into one another. Scientists then study the results. This is a way for particle physicists to study the interactions of very small particles and to determine if theoretical theories, such as supersymmetry, exist.

In 2013, the LHC announced that it had tentatively discovered a new particle scientists had long been searching for: the Higgs boson. The Higgs boson is a particle theorized in the Standard Model that might help explain the short range of the weak force. This particle could help explain some of the inconsistencies between quantum mechanics and general relativity.

While it may seem strange that a large, underground machine could do important astronomical work, this is some of the most exciting experimentation done with the Large Hadron Collider. In particular, scientists are using the collider to determine the existence of particles,

Scientists are using the Large Hadron Collider for important research in both quantum mechanics and astrophysics.

theorized using the model of supersymmetry, that could be candidates for dark matter.

According to Ben Allanach, a theoretical physicist who has worked at the Large Hadron Collider, these supersymmetric particles wouldn't be produced all that often. But, if these particles were indeed produced, some of them would decay into dark matter. Unfortunately, this doesn't mean that the LHC would necessarily be able to detect them.

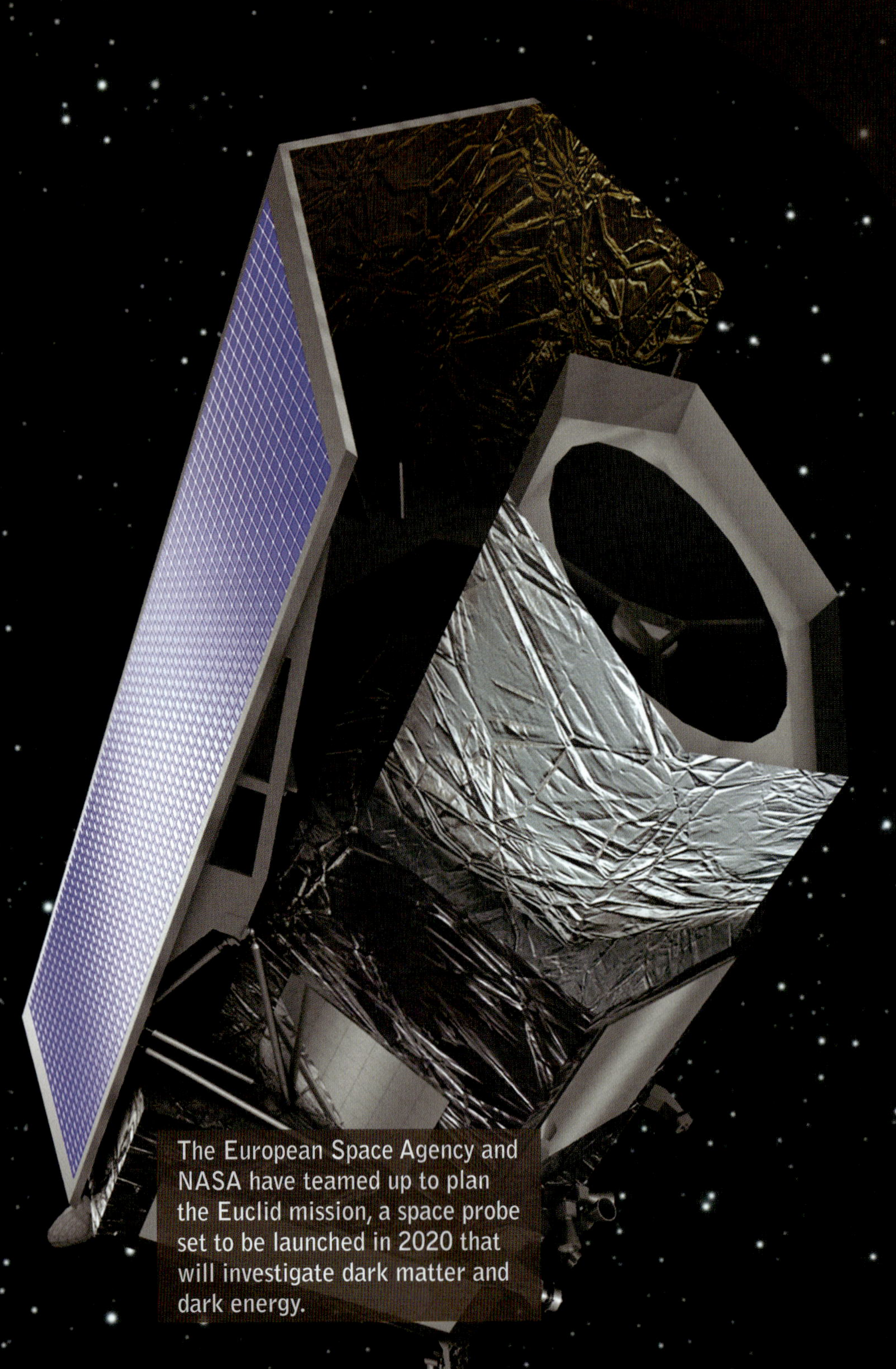

The European Space Agency and NASA have teamed up to plan the Euclid mission, a space probe set to be launched in 2020 that will investigate dark matter and dark energy.

CHAPTER 5

Dark Matter and Dark Energy Today

In the 1970s, the astronomical community was shocked with the proof of Fritz Zwicky's hypothesis that dark matter made up a large portion of the mass in our universe. Suddenly, astronomers realized that what was visible to them—not to mention what astronomers have been studying since the dawn of civilization—was only about 10 percent of all matter in the universe. This was a shocking and strange revelation. But the field of cosmology was about to get even stranger still.

Soon, astronomers would make the discovery of another unknown quantity in the universe. According to calculations, what cosmologists would name "dark energy" makes up even more of the universe than dark matter. Scientists don't yet know if there is a link between dark energy and dark matter because they don't understand the fundamentals of these quantities themselves. But, according to recent calculations, dark energy makes up 74 percent of the universe, while dark matter makes up 22 percent, and visible matter makes up only 4 percent. The amount of matter in the universe that is visible to us, astronomers believe, now makes up less than 5 percent of all existing matter!

These incredible findings were largely the result of work done by three men: Saul Perlmutter, Adam Riess, and

Brian P. Schmidt, Saul Perlmutter, and Adam G. Riess at the Breakthrough Prize Awards Ceremony in 2014

Brian Schmidt. All three men received the prestigious Nobel Prize in Physics in 2011 due to their contributions to our understanding of the universe.

OUR ACCELERATING UNIVERSE

In 1998, astrophysicist Saul Perlmutter cofounded the Supernova Cosmology Project, hoping to measure the explosions caused by dying white dwarf stars called Type 1a supernovae. Based out of Lawrence Berkeley National Laboratory in Berkeley, California, this team was composed of members across the world. Perlmutter led his team's research.

Similar to the calculations of many scientists before him, Perlmutter used the observed brightness of these supernovae to measure their distance from Earth. This is because Type 1a supernovae all form in a similar way and, thus, all have the same luminosity. Using their luminosity as a standard, Perlmutter and his team were able to calculate their distance from Earth. Then, they compared this calculated distance with the visible redshift of the supernovae. This was how they calculated the speed at which these supernovae traveled—and, thus, the speed of the universe's expansion.

As Perlmutter explained, "It seemed like my favorite kind of job—a wonderful chance to ask something absolutely fundamental: the fate of the Universe and whether the Universe was infinite or not."

At roughly the same time, another group, called the High-z Supernova Search Team, led by astronomers Adam Riess and Brian Schmidt, conducted similar research independently. This team was composed of twenty astronomers based in the United States, Europe, Australia, and Chile. Most of their observations were done at the Victor M. Blanco Telescope in Chile, Keck Observatory on the Big Island of Hawai'i, and the European Southern Observatory out of Germany. Riess, Schmidt, and their team spent years observing these distant supernovae and performing the same calculations in order to determine the expansion rate of the universe.

The leaders of both teams have stated that they did not anticipate what they would find. They believed that their research would show that distant supernovae, those farther from Earth, would be slowing down compared to closer supernovae. This was an accepted assumption many astronomers made based on the accepted consequences of the big bang: If a big explosion had propelled all of the matter in our universe outward, then it must be expanding, but also slowing down. The farther matter traveled, the more spread out it was, the less forces would act upon it—thus slowing down its speed.

Many astronomers believed that, due to the slowdown of this initial expansion outward from the big bang, our universe would end in a "**big crunch**." As the expansion of space gradually slowed down, the universe would begin to contract. This contraction would cause additional gravitational force between all the matter in the universe, causing it to collapse in on itself and forming an enormous black hole.

But both teams soon made an astounding discovery that reversed our understanding of both the forces in the universe and its fate: The distant supernovae were, in fact, traveling faster than closer supernovae. This meant that the universe was not only expanding, it was accelerating. Thus, the universe was not slowing down as astronomers had believed, but speeding up.

The similar results from both teams were published in academic journals within weeks of one another. Despite the competition between both teams, this was a good thing. In scientific inquiry, results always need to be independently verified by a re-creation of these results. If Perlmutter's team had published their results alone, it might have taken years for the scientific community to test their results and then determine that they were correct. But, since the High-z Supernova Search Team has come up with almost exactly the same results from different observations, the scientific community more readily accepted their conclusions. There was no need to wait for further proof: the universe was accelerating.

But this was just the beginning of a new problem. How was it possible for the universe to be accelerating when, according to the big bang theory, the universe should be gradually slowing down? What would cause our universe to speed up? These were the questions the astronomical community now had to ask.

Cosmologists came up with three possible explanations for this. First, they thought that it was Einstein's "cosmological constant," which he theorized in his theories of relativity as the reason why the universe had not yet collapsed into itself. Second, they thought that a liquid-like energy filled the entire universe. Finally, they imagined that there was something wrong with Einstein's theories of relativity.

Scientists are still looking for the answer to this question. In fact, we are no closer to understanding which of these possible reasons might have caused our universe to accelerate.

But, whatever the cause of this acceleration, scientists have named the force that would counteract gravitational force "dark energy"—a term coined in 1998 by the cosmologist Michael Turner.

The rest of our understanding of dark energy is largely speculative. As Adam Riess states, "Dark energy is incredibly strange, but actually it makes sense to me that it went unnoticed. I have absolutely no clue what dark energy is. Dark energy appears strong enough to push the entire universe—yet its source is unknown, its location is unknown and its physics are highly speculative."

Dark energy is responsible for the acceleration of our universe. It is invisible to all observation except for the effect it has on matter that surrounds it. Some scientists still state that dark energy, as such, can't exist. These scientists claim that, rather than dark energy, we can explain the acceleration of our universe through a completely different physical model, other than Newtonian gravity or general relativity. However, most scientists now agree that dark energy must exist—although they are still not sure what it is.

WHAT IS DARK ENERGY?

What is dark energy, then, and how does it relate to dark matter? Timothy Ferris states,

> [Astronomers have] concluded that all the stars and galaxies they see in the sky make up only 5 percent of the observable universe. The invisible majority consists of 27 percent dark matter and 68 percent dark energy. Both of them are mysteries. Dark matter is thought to be responsible for sculpting the glowing sheets and tendrils of galaxies that make up the large-scale structure of the universe—yet nobody knows what

> it is. Dark energy is even more mysterious; the term, coined to denote whatever is accelerating the rate at which the cosmos expands, has been called a "general label for what we do not know about the large-scale properties of our universe."

Michael Turner, who coined the term "dark energy," has stated that it is "the most profound mystery in all of science." After nearly two decades since the discovery of our universe's acceleration, scientists are still searching to unravel this mystery. And, while, in some ways, they might not be any closer to understanding what dark energy is than they were years earlier, in other ways, frequent scientific discoveries are continuing to close the gap of what we do know and what we do not.

NEW FRONTIERS

One project aimed at advancing our understanding is the Baryon Oscillation Spectroscopic Survey. This astronomical survey uses a telescope in New Mexico to measure distances between cosmic objects with a hitherto unknown accuracy of 99 percent. Other projects include the European Space Agency's Euclid space telescope, which is expected to launch in 2020 and will focus on mapping cosmic movements since the big bang. This, of course, will add to our understanding of how exactly, and at what rate, the expansion of the universe has been occurring.

By observing the cosmic expansion rate, astronomers will also be able to tell how the amount of dark energy in the universe has changed since the big bang. One of the consequences of this could be that our universe could continue to accelerate in its expansion until galaxies are so spread out that everything in observable range is dark matter. If this is the case, astronomers looking to the skies many, many years from now will see very little light—if any at all.

But, for now, as Ferris states, astronomers and amateurs alike have to rethink our notions of the universe. We are not surrounded by mostly empty space. In fact, we are surrounded by energy and matter that are not observable to us. In Ferris's words:

> The voids between the planets and stars were long thought to be sheer nothingness, although Isaac Newton admitted that he couldn't imagine how gravity could keep the Earth spinning around the sun if the space between them was utterly vacuous. In the 20th century, quantum field theory came to the rescue by demonstrating that space is never really empty but instead is suffused with quantum fields, which are literally everywhere. The protons, electrons, and other particles often described as the building blocks of matter are themselves excitations of quantum fields. Space looks empty when the fields languish near their minimum energy levels. But when the fields are excited, space comes alive with visible matter and energy. The mathematician Luciano Boi compares space to the water in a quiet Alpine pond: invisible when calm but evident when a breeze ripples its surface. 'Empty space is not empty,' the American physicist John Archibald Wheeler once said. 'It is the seat of the most rich and surprising physics.'

TESTING the COMPOSITION of DARK ENERGY

Astronomers have candidates for the particles that could make up dark matter, but they know even less about the strange force of dark energy. Scientists are using baryon acoustic oscillation experiments to discover more about it today. Baryons, as discussed in chapter four, are particles made from protons and neutrons. During the big bang, its force caused baryons to separate from photons. This is what caused the cosmic microwave background—the most important evidence for the big bang even today—and allows astronomers to hear the sound waves caused from the birth of our universe. If astronomers focus on this cosmic microwave background, they can study how it has changed over time. This is because peaks in these oscillations illustrate when regions of the universe were especially dense. Comparing these peaks will tell astronomers the rate of expansion of the universe and will shed some light on how dark energy has developed and grown.

Gravitational Lensing

Another way scientists are currently investigating dark energy is through something called gravitational lensing. Gravitational lensing is a phenomenon that arises from Einstein's general theory of relativity: it describes how a beam of light bends when it enters into the field of gravity of a certain mass, which is due, in fact, not to the light's own movement so much as the bending of space.

Using gravitational lensing, scientists can study clusters of galaxies that are grouped one in front of another. The light from the galaxies in the background will be distorted as it passes around the galaxies in front of it. By measuring this distortion, astronomers can measure the mass of the galaxy closest to them.

Galaxy clusters, in fact, are an important source of information for astronomers searching for answers about dark energy. This is because scientists who study these dense pockets of the universe over time will be able to tell if any changes are occurring. If areas of the universe become less dense or, rather, filled less with visible matter, this is a good indication that the concentration of dark energy is shifting as well.

The gravity of a large red galaxy is shown to distort the light from a distant blue galaxy in this photo showing gravitational lensing.

Testing General Relativity

Of course, astronomical studies of dark energy are based on the assumption that we know how gravity works. However, many physicists and other scientists—including Einstein himself toward the end of his life—believe that our understanding of gravitational forces is limited. This is due to scientists' inability to reconcile the physics of quantum mechanics with the theory of general relativity. As Ferris states:

> Dark energy may prove him to have been prophetic on the largest possible scale. To understand how cosmic space balloons—and why it now seems to be ballooning ever faster—physicists rely mainly on Einstein's general theory of relativity, composed a century ago. That theory works well on the large scale but bows out at the microscopic level, where quantum theory reigns and the underlying cause of accelerating cosmic expansion is thought to reside. Explaining dark energy may require something new: a quantum theory of space and gravitation.

To do this, physicists are conducting a range of experiments today to test Einstein's theory. When the Apollo 11 mission landed on the moon in 1969, the astronauts brought with them reflective panels. Since then, more panels have been installed. Scientists today aim lasers at the moon and wait for the light to bounce back, which should take approximately 2.5 seconds. Using this information, astronomers are able to calculate to the greatest possible accuracy the distances between Earth and the moon.

Why is measuring this distance important for our understanding of dark matter and dark energy? Because if there is any deviation between calculations in the moon's orbit due to gravitational forces, according to general relativity, and what is observable through these experiments, then we will know that Einstein's general theory of relativity does not hold up. So far, however, Einstein's calculations remain correct more than a hundred years later.

Concurrently, other groups of scientists have been studying the way gravity works in extremely close range. Today, scientists have measured distances between small objects that are separated by only tiny distances—for example, 56 microns, which is approximately 1/500 of an inch. The experimenters then compare this measured distance with what general relativity predicts. So far, these numbers are exactly the same, illustrating that general relativity remains our best understanding of gravitational forces that we have today.

One of the scientific leaders of the quest to reconcile general relativity and quantum mechanics is a well-known figure to most: Stephen Hawking. In 1974, Hawking's work on so-called Hawking radiation, or subatomic particles that are radiated by black holes, shows the confluence of general relativity, in the large phenomena of the black hole, and quantum mechanics, in the subatomic particles that are emitted due to quantum effects. Hawking has continued to work toward this "theory of everything." His work on string theory, in particular, which postulates that all particles are composed of tiny strings of matter that vibrate, seems a promising inquiry into quantum gravity, or the way gravity works on a tiny scale.

Gravitational Waves

Another prediction that Einstein's theories of relativity made was that waves could travel in the force of gravity as they could travel through air. According to Einstein, "these gravitational waves are formed when masses move back and forth in space-time, much as sound waves are created by the oscillations of a speaker cone." This was shown to be true in 1974, when scientists discovered two stars that orbited around one another. The stars were both losing a small amount of mass that was exactly as calculated using Einstein's formula. In fact, the gravity created by these two stars formed gravitational waves that radiated away from them. The small amount of mass that was lost had been converted to the energy found in these gravitational waves.

At the beginning of 2016, physicists at the Laser Interferometer Gravitational-Wave Observatory (LIGO) announced that they had detected the first proof of gravitational waves. Finally, this last prediction in general relativity was tested—and shown to exist. The significance of this discovery is only starting to unravel. In the future, gravitational-wave astronomy will be an important branch of cosmology and will lead the way to new discoveries as astronomers use measurements of gravitational waves to answer questions about dark matter and dark energy.

EINSTEIN'S COSMOLOGICAL CONSTANT and QUINTESSENCE

Today, many cosmologists have two main theories of what dark energy could be. On a theoretical level, cosmologists either believe that dark energy reflects Einstein's cosmological constant, which was part of his original theory of general relativity, or a theory called quintessence.

Those who point to Einstein's original cosmological constant believe that general relativity is an incredibly accurate theory that not only withstands the existence of dark matter and dark energy, but actually predicted it! In 1917, when Einstein first developed his theory, he included the cosmological constant in his calculations of general relativity before Hubble's discovery of the expansion of the universe. Although Einstein later referred to the cosmological constant as his biggest mistake, scientists today point to the fact that the cosmological constant could be the best fit for dark energy that we know of today.

According to Einstein, supposedly "empty" space has its own energy. As the universe expands outward from the big bang, this energy—evenly distributed through space because it is in the nature of space itself—would grow and grow, causing space to accelerate in its expansion. This would cause an almost infinite cycle of expansion, increased energy, and then increased expansion. If this theory is correct, dark energy has always existed and will always continue to exist. This theoretical understanding of dark energy, however, does not explain the nature of dark energy or of its interactions—which scientists are still trying to understand.

Other scientists believe in something called quintessence. Quintessence is named after the ancient Greek word that described a fifth element after air, earth, fire, and water, that allowed celestial bodies to remain fixed in the sky. According to scientists who believe in this theory, quintessence (another word to describe dark energy according to this theory) is a quantum field that was created relatively recently:

> Quintessence became a force to be reckoned with about 10 billion years ago, according to the theory. That may seem rather early on in a 15 billion-year-old universe, but cosmologists don't see it that way. The

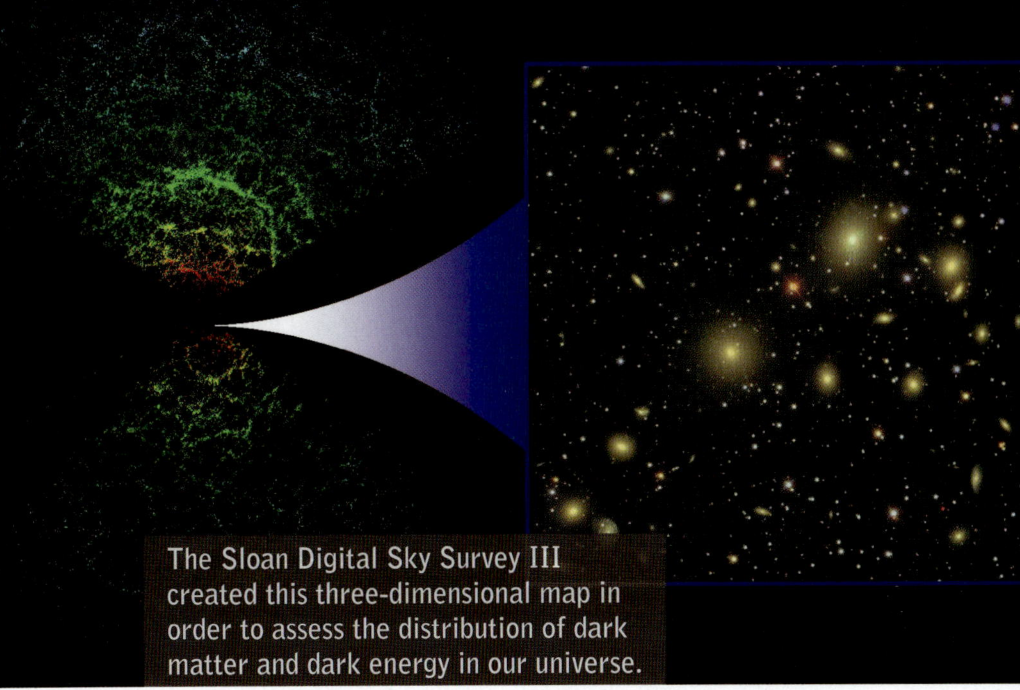

The Sloan Digital Sky Survey III created this three-dimensional map in order to assess the distribution of dark matter and dark energy in our universe.

dark energy was created when the universe was 10^{-35} second old; it did not cause the universe to accelerate for another five billion years. That's a factor of more than 10^{50}—and relatively recently in terms of redshift and the size of the universe.

The creation of quintessence began when the early universe transitioned from being composed of mostly radiation, to being filled with matter. Proponents of this theory believe that quintessence changes over time and interacts with matter, which means that the universe will not expand out infinitely. According to Paul Steinhardt, an astrophysicist and proponent of quintessence at Princeton University, this is why quintessence is a stronger theory than the cosmological constant:

> The cosmological constant is a very specific form of energy, a vacuum energy. Quintessence encompasses a wide class of possibilities. It is a dynamic, time-evolving and spatially dependent form of energy with negative pressure sufficient to drive the accelerating expansion.

Despite the strengths of the theory of quintessence, however, most cosmologists today have not yet accepted it. The theory would still fit in with Einstein's theory of general relativity, but there are still many unknowns that need to be answered before scientist would be willing to accept the existence of quintessence.

In order to test such theories, Saul Perlmutter, who originally discovered the existence of the acceleration of the universe, is leading the Supernova Acceleration Project (SNAP). SNAP uses a satellite with a 2-meter (6.5-foot) telescope to find distant supernovae that land-based telescopes would not be able to find. This is especially exciting because the satellite would be able to find and calculate the redshifts on more than two thousand distant supernovae a year—thus, further clarifying the exact speed of acceleration of our universe. This project is expected to be launched in 2020.

The UNIFIED FIELD THEORY

Albert Einstein spent most of his life trying to understand how gravity affects both very large objects and very small objects similarly and, thus, reconciling general relativity and quantum mechanics. General relativity allowed Einstein to reimagine space as space-time, which responded by bending to mass or energy. If Einstein was able to understand how small atomic particles acted geometrically in similar ways, then general relativity would not only be applicable to very large objects in space but also to the tiny particles in the world of quantum mechanics.

Einstein called this the unified field theory, and he searched for it, fruitlessly, for the rest of his life. Back in the 1920s, when Einstein was attempting to reconcile electromagnetism with general relativity, scientists had just discovered quantum mechanics. They didn't know of any other subatomic particles besides the proton and the electron. They also hadn't yet discovered forces beyond electromagnetism and gravity (such as the weak nuclear force, which is responsible for radioactive decay of subatomic particles, and the strong nuclear force, which binds protons and neutrons together in atoms). Many scientists were confused as to why Einstein wanted to reconcile these two different forces, but Einstein strongly believed that two separate and independent fields could not govern nature. In a speech he gave after winning the Nobel Prize in 1922, Einstein stated: "The intellect seeking after an integrated theory cannot rest content with the assumption that there exist two distinct fields totally independent of each other by their nature."

Today, scientists still struggle with a unified field theory, also known as the grand unified theory (GUT; to describe the unification of all forces besides gravity) or "the theory of everything" (to describe the unification of all forces including gravity). Many scientists have contributed importantly to understanding how these interactions can be described in terms of a single field, but these four forces have not yet been understood all together. Gravitational force, in particular, is hard to incorporate with the other interactions. Today, more than one hundred years since the publication of Einstein's theory of general relativity, scientists have still been unable to reconcile general relativity and quantum mechanics into a single and consistent theory.

Why is quantum mechanics important to the field of astronomy? Quantum physics applies to "singularity" phenomena like black holes, which are really just an extreme blackbody, like the blackbodies Planck tested when he first discovered the wave-particle duality of light. It is also useful to studies of the behavior of some kinds of stars, such as neutron stars and white dwarfs. More importantly, many astronomers and physicists believe that the key to understanding dark energy will be in discovering this "theory of everything." Most astronomers do agree that the most important mysteries in astronomy—the existence of dark matter and dark energy—must be tied to the greatest challenge in physics—the reconciliation of quantum mechanics and general relativity.

While some physicists today disregard Einstein's lifelong search for a unification theory as misdirected and even wrong, many continue to dedicate their life's work to finding the underlying theory that could explain these various forces. These physicists and astronomers claim that, at the moment of the big bang and immediately after, these four forces were one—before they were ripped apart and became distinct. Understanding the physical law that would govern—and explain the interactions of—all of these forces would help us to better understand the outstanding mysteries of our universe.

ONWARDS, SPACE PIONEERS!

For many readers, it may seem frustrating that, despite the exciting discoveries of dark matter and dark energy over the past forty years, we still know little about what exactly these strange quantities are. As Timothy Ferris states:

> Scientists are confronted by the embarrassing fact that they don't know just how much energy, dark or otherwise, space contains. When quantum theorists try to calculate how much energy resides in, say, a quart of seemingly empty space, they get a big number. But astronomers calculating the same quantity from their dark energy observations get a small number. The difference between the two numbers is staggering: It's ten to the 121st power, a one followed by 121 zeroes, an amount far exceeding the number of stars in the observable universe or grains of sand on the planet. That's the largest disparity between theory and observation in the entire history of science. Clearly something fundamentally important about space—and therefore about everything, since galaxies, stars, planets, and people are made mostly of space—remains to be learned.

Despite our lack of knowledge about the details involving the composition and interactions of dark matter and dark energy—as well as the larger problem, referenced by Ferris, of reconciling quantum mechanics and general relativity—this is a very exciting time for cosmologists and astrophysicists. Astronomy is the continual pursuit of answers to our fundamental questions, and, often, astronomers expect the solving of one question to lead to many more questions. As Vera Rubin states, the posing of each new question lights up a brief spark in a dark room. The accumulation of many curious minds asking many questions can be the equivalent of a lightbulb that flashes for just a second before dimming. This might not seem like much, but a brief second of light allows humans to look around, however quickly, and see clearly for just that instant. And isn't that a wonderful thing? With each new question, with each new technological development and each new inquisitive mind, this brightness will grow.

Vera Rubin, one of the greatest minds of astronomy, urges new minds to contribute to the field that she revolutionized:

> Less than 400 years ago Galileo put a small lens at one end of a cardboard tube and a big brain at the other end. In so doing, he learned that the faint stripe across the sky, called the Milky Way, in fact comprised billions of single stars and stellar clusters. Suddenly, a human being understood what a galaxy is. Perhaps in the coming century, another—as yet unborn—big brain will put her eye to a clever new instrument and definitively answer, What is dark matter?

You, too, can ask these big questions—and maybe, one day, answer them, too. Why? As Rubin rightly states, "Each one of you can change the world, for you are made of star stuff, and you are connected to the universe."

Reworking Gravity?

Some scientists have tried to rethink how gravity works among large objects in space in order to explain the existence of dark matter and dark energy. In 1983, an Israeli physicist named Mordehai Milgrom attempted to explain why the velocity of stars was larger than it should be. He postulated a theory called modified Newtonian dynamics (MOND), which revises **Newton's second law** and modifies how gravity works with large celestial objects.

This, however, would not only turn Newtonian gravity on its head—but also Einstein's general relativity. While MOND has had some success in predicting the motion and speed of some galaxies, scientists still aren't on board with the theory. Most scientists believe, rather, that dark matter exists and adds mass to our universe. Scientists who believe in MOND, however, believe that dark matter and dark energy do not exist, but that our understanding of gravity is incomplete and that the laws themselves need to be revised.

The reason why many scientists have not given much credence to MOND is because of a principle called Occam's razor. Occam's razor is a philosophical theory that the simplest explanation for something is usually the best explanation. This doesn't mean that scientists don't pursue very complex solutions—far from it, in fact. However, scientists usually prefer building on and improving existing theories, rather than destroying existing models and starting from scratch, partly because the simpler answers are easier to test and observe. Most astronomers have not adopted the theory of modified Newtonian dynamics because it would throw away most of what we know about both Newtonian gravity and the general theory of relativity—essentially, leaving scientists with even larger questions.

Chronology

1785 William Herschel first maps out the Milky Way galaxy, with our own solar system at the center.

1900 Max Planck investigates blackbody surfaces and concludes that colors (light) are emitted in packets called quanta. This is the beginning of quantum mechanics.

1905 Albert Einstein calls these packets of light "photons" and declares that they exhibit wave-particle duality.

1913 Veso Slipher first uses the Doppler effect to determine that nebulae are moving away from Earth at incredible speeds.

1915 Einstein first publishes his general theory of relativity and revolutionizes the field of physics.

1917 Einstein adds the cosmological constant to his calculations in general relativity, in order to show a "static" universe. He later calls this his biggest blunder.

1920 The Great Debate occurs between Harlow Shapley and Heber Curtis over whether the Milky Way is the only galaxy in the universe.

1923 Edwin Hubble takes exposures of the Andromeda galaxy in October, which lead him to discover that our universe is previously larger than ever imagined.

1926 Hubble calculates the size of the universe and shows that everything in space is rapidly moving away from Earth. This is known as Hubble's law.

1927 In an obscure paper, Georges Lemaître shows the connection between Einstein's general theory of relativity and the expanding universe.

1931 Although he doesn't call it the big bang, Lemaître states that there must have been a big explosion at the birth of our universe. This is hotly debated for many years.

1932 Fritz Zwicky states that "dark matter" could explain the missing mass in galaxy clusters that prevents them from flying apart.

1949 The term "big bang" is coined, although this theory will not be accepted by most astronomers until proof of cosmic background radiation is found in 1964.

1958 Allan Sandage, Edwin Hubble's student, more accurately calculates the rate of expansion of the universe, which he calls the Hubble constant.

1964 Two radio astronomers, Arno Penzias and Robert Woodrow Wilson, accidently discover cosmic background radiation, proof of the big bang. They will win the Nobel Prize in 1974 for their discovery.

1978 Vera Rubin and Kent Ford use a spectrometer to calculate the Doppler shift of galaxies; due to the surprising speeds of these galaxies, they prove the existence of dark matter.

1998 Saul Perlmutter, leading the Supernova Cosmology Project, and Adam Riess and Brian Schmidt, of the High-z Supernova Search Team, both publish papers showing that the universe is rapidly accelerating.

2011 Saul Perlmutter, Adam Riess, and Brian Schmidt win the Nobel Prize in Physics for their discovery that the universe is accelerating.

Glossary

astrolabe An instrument, or early computer, used to take astronomical measurements to calculate time and latitude.

astrophysics A branch of study that uses physics and mathematical calculations to understand the birth, life, and death of celestial objects, as well as the fundamental forces present in the universe.

baryon A composite subatomic particle, which includes protons and neutrons, that makes up most of the mass of visible matter in our universe.

big crunch The possible scenario that our universe will gradually slow down and contract in on itself, causing a massive black hole.

blackbody radiation The electromagnetic radiation emitted from a nonreflective body.

black hole An incredibly dense area of space-time that exerts such gravitational force that no radiation can escape from it.

Cepheid variable star A kind of very bright star that pulsates in predictable ways.

cosmic microwave background radiation (CMB) Thermal radiation left over from the big bang.

cosmological constant Einstein's original value of the energy of space, which he later deleted following Hubble's discovery of the expansion of the universe. However, many scientists today believe that the cosmological constant could explain the existence of dark energy.

cosmology The science of the origin and evolution of the universe; a branch of astronomy.

Doppler shift The change in frequency of a wave depending on whether an object is moving toward or away from an observer.

experimentum crucius Latin for "crucial experiment," this is an experiment that determines whether or not a theory is correct.

feedback loop The path by which the output of a system is fed back into the system.

galaxy A system of many stars, along with gas and dust, that is held together by gravitational forces.

galaxy cluster A group of galaxies that are bound together by gravitational forces.

Great Debate In astronomy, the debate between astronomers Harlow Shapley and Heber Curtis over whether the universe was composed of one galaxy or many.

Hubble constant The unit of measurement used to determine the expansion of the universe.

Hubble's law A law that states that the rate at which astronomical objects move apart from each other is proportional to their distance from each other.

irregular galaxy A galaxy that does not have a regular shape, such as an ellipse or a spiral, and is mostly composed of young stars and large amounts of gas and dust.

luminosity In physics, the rate of emission of radiation.

massive compact halo object (MACHO) Normal baryonic matter that scientists once believed could make up dark matter; this has been largely disproven.

nebula A cloud of gas or dust in the universe.

Newton's second law A law that states that the acceleration of an object is directly proportional to the magnitude of the force that produced this acceleration, inversely proportional to the mass of the object, and moves in the same direction.

nomenclature The process of naming something or the system of names in a particular field.

particle collider Otherwise known as a particle accelerator, this machine uses electromagnetic fields to propel charged particles to nearly light speed.

pulsation pattern To expand or contract rhythmically; in astronomy, the patterned luminosity of certain stars.

quanta A small packet of energy or charge.

radioactive decay When an unstable atomic nuclear is changed into a lighter one, thus releasing energy in the form of radiation.

space-time According to Einstein's general theory of relativity, the belief that the fabric of our universe is composed of both time and the three dimensions of space.

spectrograph (or spectrometer) An apparatus for recording and measuring spectra, or bands of colors.

speed of light A physical constant at which rate electromagnetic radiation travels in a vacuum.

Standard Model of physics A theory of the four fundamental physical forces, as well as all of the known atomic and subatomic particles.

supernova A star that suddenly increases in brightness due to an explosion at the end of its life.

supersymmetry An as-of-yet unproven physical theory in which all particles have symmetric partners.

uncertainty principle In quantum mechanics, the principle that the momentum and position of a particle cannot both be known at the same time.

vacuum A space devoid of all matter and forces.

virial theorem An important mathematical theorem that states that the kinetic energy of certain objects must equal the kinetic energy, within a factor of two.

weakly interacting massive particles (WIMPs) Hypothetical non-baryonic particles that are a potential candidate for dark matter.

white dwarf star Medium-sized star at the end of its life cycle that exhausts all of its nuclear fuel.

wormhole A hypothetical passage in space-time, postulated by Albert Einstein in his theory of general relativity, that could create shortcuts from one area of the universe to another.

Further Information

BOOKS

Gates Evalyn. *Einstein's Telescope: The Hunt for Dark Matter and Dark Energy in the Universe*. New York: W. W. Norton, 2009.

Panek, Richard. *The 4% Universe: Dark Matter, Dark Energy, and the Race to Discover the Rest of Reality*. New York: Mariner Books, 2011.

Randall, Lisa. *Dark Matter and Dinosaurs: The Astounding Interconnectedness of the Universe*. New York: Ecco, 2015.

WEBSITES

Dark Energy, Dark Matter: NASA Science
science.nasa.gov/astrophysics/focus-areas/what-is-dark-energy/

The National Aeronautics and Space Administration (NASA) dedicates this page to basic information about dark matter and dark energy, as well as an updated list of recent discoveries.

Hubble Site: Dark Energy
hubblesite.org/hubble_discoveries/dark_energy/

An interactive video about dark energy leads viewers into educational topics about the discovery of dark energy, Einstein's cosmological constant, and Type 1a supernovae.

UC Berkeley Cosmology Group: Dark Matter and Related FAQs
cosmology.berkeley.edu/Education/FAQ/faq.html

Leading cosmologists at the UC Berkeley Cosmology Group have answered questions about dark matter and dark energy and listed their responses here.

ORGANIZATIONS

Caltech Astronomy
www.astro.caltech.edu/

This is Caltech Astronomy's homepage, which includes the names of leading researchers and their current research, news, and events.

CERN: The Large Hadron Collider
home.cern/topics/large-hadron-collider

The European Organization for Nuclear Research (CERN) houses the Large Hadron Collider. Here, you can find information about how the largest particle accelerator works, see pictures and videos of the LHC and its building, and read recent news about work done here.

Lawrence Berkeley National Laboratory: Supernova Acceleration Probe
snap.lbl.gov/science/how.php

The official website for the Supernova Acceleration Probe (SNAP) describes dark energy, Saul Perlmutter's project to launch a probe to find distant supernovae, and technical information about the probe.

Bibliography

ABC Melbourne. "Nobel Prize Winner Professor Brian Schmidt." October 5, 2011 (http://www.abc.net.au/local/stories/2011/10/05/3332822.htm).

American Physical Society. "Einstein's Quest for a Unified Theory." APS News, December 2005 (https://www.aps.org/publications/apsnews/200512/history.cfm).

Annenberg Learner. "Dark Matter in the Early Universe." Physics for the 12st Century (https://www.learner.org/courses/physics/unit/text.html?unit=10&secNum=3).

Bartusiak, Marcia. *The Day We Found the Universe*. New York: Vintage Books, 2009.

Brookhaven National Laboratory. "New Theory of Secondary Inflation Expands Options for Avoiding an Excess of Dark Matter." January 14, 2016 (https://www.bnl.gov/newsroom/news.php?a=11805).

CERN. "The Large Hadron Collider" (http://home.cern/topics/large-hadron-collider).

Cooper, Keith. "Allan Sandage, 1926–2010." *Astronomy Now*, November 16, 2010 (http://www.astronomynow.com/news/n1011/16Sandage).

Daily Galaxy. "The Dark Energy Enigma—'The Entire Universe Is Being Pushed by an Unknown Force No One Can Locate." January 30, 2016 (http://www.dailygalaxy.com/my_weblog/2016/01/-the-dark-energy-mystery-the-entire-universe-is-being-pushed-by-an-invisible-unknown-force-no-one-ca.html).

Diemand, Jürg. "Milky Way's Dark Matter Halo." Solstation (http://www.solstation.com/x-objects/darkhalo.htm).

Doyle, Laurance R. "Quantum Astronomy: The Double Slit Experiment." Space.com, November 11, 2004 (http://www.space.com/529-quantum-astronomy-double-slit-experiment.html).

Ferris, Timothy. "A First Glimpse of the Hidden Cosmos." *National Geographic*, January 2015 (http://ngm.nationalgeographic.com/print/2015/01/hidden-cosmos/ferris-text).

Halpern, Paul. *Einstein's Dice and Schrodinger's Cat: How Two Great Minds Battled Quantum Randomness to Create a Unified Theory of Physics*. New York; Basic Books, 2015.

Krauss, Lawrence M. *A Universe from Nothing: Why There Is Something Rather Than Nothing*. New York: Simon and Schuster, 2012.

Kucharski, Adam. "Relativity's Long String of Successful Predictions." *Discover Magazine*, March 10, 2015 (http://discovermagazine.com/2015/april/12-putting-relativity-to-the-test).

Larsen, Kristen. "Vera Cooper Rubin." *Jewish Women's Archive* (http://jwa.org/encyclopedia/article/rubin-vera-cooper).

Levy, David H., and Wendy Wallach-Levy. *Cosmic Discoveries*. New York: Prometheus Books, 2001.

Mann, Adam. "Supersymmetry: The Future of Physics Explained." *Wired*, July 2, 2012 (http://www.wired.com/2012/07/supersymmetry-explained).

Mastin, Luke. "Important Scientists: Arthur Eddington (1882–1944)." The Physics of the Universe, 2009 (http://www.physicsoftheuniverse.com/scientists_eddington.html).

Mastin, Luke. "Important Scientists: Georges Lemaître (1894–1966)." The Physics of the Universe, 2009 (http://www.physicsoftheuniverse.com/scientists_lemaitre.html).

Mastin, Luke. "Main Topics: Black Holes and Wormholes." The Physics of the Universe, 2009 (http://www.physicsoftheuniverse.com/topics_blackholes_wormholes.html).

Net Industries. "Gravity and Gravitation—General Relativity." 2016 (http://science.jrank.org/pages/3131/Gravity-Gravitation-General-relativity.html).

Nobelprize.org. "The Nobel Prize in Physics 2011 Press Release." October 4, 2011 (http://www.nobelprize.org/nobel_prizes/physics/laureates/2011/press.html).

Norton, John D. "Einstein of the Completeness of Quantum Theory." Einstein for Everyone. Department of History and Philosophy of Science, University of Pittsburgh (http://www.pitt.edu/~jdnorton/teaching/HPS_0410/chapters_2015_Jan_1/quantum_theory_completeness/index.html).

Observations of the Carnegie Institution for Science."1917: Albert Einstein Invents the Cosmological Constant" (https://cosmology.carnegiescience.edu/timeline/1917).

O'Neill, Ian. "Dark Matter Just Got Darker (and Weirder)." Discovery, March 26, 2015 (http://news.discovery.com/space/galaxies/dark-matter-just-got-darker-and-weirder-150326.htm).

O'Neill, Ian. "Wait a Minute, Dark Matter May Not be Dark After All." Discovery, April 14, 2015 (http://news.discovery.com/space/galaxies/wait-just-a-minute-dark-matter-may-not-be-dark-after-all-150414.htm).

Palmer, Jason. "Nobel Physics Prize Honours Accelerating Universe Find." BBC News, October 4, 2011 (http://www.bbc.com/news/science-environment-15165371).

Panek, Richard. "Dark Energy: The Biggest Mystery in the Universe." *Smithsonian Magazine*, April 2010 (http://www.smithsonianmag.com/science-nature/dark-energy-the-biggest-mystery-in-the-universe-9482130/?page=4).

Panek, Richard. "The Father of Dark Matter Still Gets No Respect." *Discover Magazine*, January 2009 (http://discovermagazine.com/2009/jan/30-the-father-of-dark-matter-still-gets-no-respect).

Pearson, Chris. "Fundamental Cosmology: 4. General Relativistic Cosmology." ISAS, November 2, 2003 (http://www.ir.isas.jaxa.jp/~cpp/teaching/cosmology/documents/cosmology01-04.pdf).

Rubin, Vera. "Dark Matter in the Universe." *Scientific American*, 1998 (http://www2.lbl.gov/Science-Articles/Archive/sabl/2006/Jan/Rubin-Dark-Matter.pdf).

Sagan, Carl. "A Pale Blue Dot: Excerpt from *Pale Blue Dot* (1994)." The Planetary Society (http://www.planetary.org/explore/space-topics/earth/pale-blue-dot.html).

Singh, Simon. "Even Einstein Had His Off Days." *New York Times*, January 2, 2005 (http://www.nytimes.com/2005/01/02/opinion/even-einstein-had-his-off-days.html).

Soter, Steven, and Neil deGrasse Tyson, eds. "Vera Rubin and Dark Matter." Excerpt from *Cosmic Horizons: Astronomy at the Cutting Edge*, American Museum of Natural History,

2000 (http://www.amnh.org/education/resources/rfl/web/essaybooks/cosmic/p_rubin.html).

Soter, Steven, and Neil deGrasse Tyson, eds. "Georges Lemaître: Father of the Big Bang." Excerpt from *Cosmic Horizons: Astronomy at the Cutting Edge*, American Museum of Natural History, 2000 (http://www.amnh.org/education/resources/rfl/web/essaybooks/cosmic/p_lemaitre.html

Strassler, Matt. "Supersymmetry—What Is It?" Of Particular Significance: Conversations About Science with Theoretical Physicist Matt Strassler (http://profmattstrassler.com/articles-and-posts/some-speculative-theoretical-ideas-for-the-lhc/supersymmetry/supersymmetry-what-is-it)

Straumann, Norbert. "Fritz Zwicky: An Extraordinary Astrophysicist." Swiss Physical Society (http://www.sps.ch/en/articles/history-of-physics/fritz-zwicky-an-extraordinary-astrophysicist-6).

Thims, Libb, *Human Chemistry, Vol. 1*. Lulu.com, 2007.

Tyson, Peter. "The Legacy of $E=mc^2$." *NOVA*, October 1,1 2015 (http://www.pbs.org/wgbh/nova/physics/legacy-of-e-equals-mc2.html).

Wanjek, Christopher. "Quintessence, Accelerating the Universe?" Astronomy Today (http://www.astronomytoday.com/cosmology/quintessence.html).

Wheeler, John A. "Information, Physics, Quantum: The Search for Links." In *Complexity, Entropy, and the Physics of Information*, Wojciech Hubert Zurek, ed. Redwood City, California: Addison-Wesley, 1990.

Williams, Alicia, and Chenise Williams. "Vera Rubin—Astronomer." Quotabelle, August 2015 (http://www.quotabelle.com/author/vera-rubin).

Index

Page numbers in **boldface** are illustrations. Entries in **boldface** are glossary terms.

About the Author

Elizabeth Schmermund is a writer, scholar, and editor. While her days are mostly filled with literature—and not necessarily astronomical study—she has always had a great curiosity about astronomy and physics. At one time, she planned to graduate with a degree in astronomy and even had the opportunity to conduct research at Kitt Peak in Arizona and the Mauna Kea Observatories on the Big Island of Hawaii. Today, she has a telescope and loves staring out at the planets and stars with her husband and young son. She credits Carl Sagan with initiating her love of astronomy at a young age.